"Variety, yes, but th different woman. The va creativity a woman and m.... ... .

Holding his gaze, she said, "I'd like very much to test out my creativity with you."

The words fell into the deepest, darkest silence, the kind where all the voices fade, the laughter mutes – the moment between life and death, love and hate, yes and no.

He felt it too, and drew it out until finally he exhaled.

"I thought you'd never ask."

More Than A Night

By

Jasmine Haynes

Liquid Silver Books
Indianapolis, Indiana

This is a work of fiction. The characters, incidents, and dialogues in this book are products of the author's imagination and are not to be construed as real. Any resemblance to actual events or persons, living or dead, is entirely coincidental..

Published By:
Liquid Silver Books
6280 Crittenden Ave.
Indianapolis, IN 46220

Liquid Silver Books publishes books online and in trade paperback. Visit our site at http://www.liquidsilverbooks.com

Manufactured in the United States of America

ISBN: 1-931761-66-3

Cover: Shirley A. Schult

More Than A Night

CHAPTER ONE

Justine Jarreau wanted a man. But only for the night.

She'd found her quarry seated two tables away. The trendy but casual restaurant on Union Square overflowed with tourists, out-of-town businessmen, clubbers from the suburbs out to enjoy San Francisco nightlife on a warm June Friday.

The mandatory package of condoms lounged in her purse.

Not classically handsome, the man bore a square jaw, strong lines, and thick, short brown hair. She liked short hair. The rugged lines at his mouth and his tan were manufactured out-of-doors rather than in a tanning booth. Muscles bulged beneath his black polo shirt.

As he'd passed her table on the way to his, she'd noted that the rear view was equally scintillating. Mid-thirties, she judged. Well-tended body. Excellent. Neither inexperience nor sloppiness was on her list of attributes.

His looks alone didn't make him the best candidate for the evening. It was the glass he'd sent to her table, a chardonnay, right as she'd finished her first.

A woman likes to be noticed, especially dressed as she was in a short skirt, tight knit top, and four-inch killer heels. Her strawberry blonde hair curled softly at her shoulders.

Better yet, a woman likes subtlety. He'd tipped his drink to her as she'd sipped. And that was all. No harassment, no asking to join her, no swaggering dickhead mentality. Just a compliment.

And an unspoken invitation, if she chose to take him up on it. Which she most definitely would.

He called for his check. She signaled for hers. After signing the charge slip, he laid his money down for the tip and rose to leave, with one last smile for Justine.

She caught up with him outside, on the sidewalk rippling with excitement. A rich coffee scent drifted out from the café next to the restaurant, effectively dousing the car fumes from the street. The June evening had grown muggy with the purr of car engines belching exhaust, yet goose bumps pimpled her bare legs.

Maybe it was the realization that she'd actually have to make the next move.

"Excuse me."

He turned and smiled as if he'd been waiting for her.

God. She'd thought him attractive inside, but up close, he was melt-in-your-mouth gorgeous. It was the eyes, a deep brown as rich as the coffee perfuming the air. Long dark eyelashes and a smile hot enough to make her heart flutter capped it. She was almost afraid to hear his voice in case it ruined the fantasy.

Her knees weakened with the knowledge that she'd never done anything like this before. She'd struggled through relationships, sure, but found they only got in the way of her career. And her career was more important than anything.

The concept of a one-night-stand was somehow liberating.

"Thank you for the drink. Can I buy you one in return?"

His eyes darkened to deep chocolate. "It would be my pleasure to accept."

Justine liquefied. He had a phone sex voice, low, deep, toe-curling.

"My hotel's across the street," he went on. "Good jazz piano in the bar."

An out-of-towner. Good. Very good. She checked his ring finger for a telltale band of white skin. She wanted a man with no strings attached. Even if this was just for a night, she didn't want to poach on someone else's territory.

She smiled, giving him a slow, sexy dip of her eyelashes. "Sounds perfect."

He took her hand unexpectedly. Warm. Solid. She had to catch her breath against the jolt of his touch. Pins and needles tingled along her skin. She felt naked beneath her skirt, and warm, oh so warm, right in that spot … there. She almost sighed.

"My name's Justine," she told him as he pulled her close, almost protectively, threading through the stopped traffic.

On the opposite curb, he looked down at her eyes, her lips, and finally their clasped hands. The moment before she couldn't breathe, now, her heart seemed to stop altogether.

"Len," was all he said with an electrifying smile, but he might have been citing flowery poetry or talking dirty for the effect it had on her.

The man made her absolutely hot. And wet. God.

The St. George doorman ushered them through the gold-trimmed entrance. Her heels sunk into the lush rose carpet as the man named Len guided her up the stairs to the lobby. Plush chairs and sofas surrounded by ferns dotted the reception area. Women clad in elegant evening wear and men in tuxedos undulated in flowing groups near the restaurant entrance.

Theater-goers filled the bar, having a drink and a gossip before the show. The piano bench sat empty due to the early hour. The city didn't truly come alive until after nine.

Len waved a bill, and the waiter found them a table in the corner by the window overlooking Powell Street. Justine curled her legs beneath her on the bench seat and leaned an elbow along the back.

"I love watching people," she said, letting Len order the drinks, Campari and soda for him, another glass of wine for her. "That's what I like best about living in the city." She turned to him. "Are you here on business?"

"Just for the day. I'm driving back tomorrow."

Their drinks arrived. Len tapped his to hers and drank. She had the urge to lick the bitter Campari from his lips.

Ostensibly to hear her better over the din of voices and laughter, he pulled his chair closer until his knee rested against hers. The contact pulsed along her thighs. She'd worn a bra, but he couldn't avoid noticing her nipples peaking against the thin lace.

"I take it you live in the city?" he questioned. "Do you work here, too?"

"No, I work on the Peninsula." That was the thing she hated about the city, the grinding commute south, the endless rush hour. "I'm Controller for a small manufacturing firm."

His eyes grazed her tight shirt, short skirt and bare knees. Then the corner of his mouth lifted.

"You don't look like any accountant I've ever met."

Her gaze followed the muscles of his chest down to the flatness of his abdomen, then onto the tight lines of his black jeans outlining the promise of some very tasty equipment. Heat suddenly burned between her legs.

She really had let sex go for too long, way too long.

"And you don't look like a ... shoe salesman from Muncie."

He laughed, a sound she felt low in her belly.

"Thank you, ma'am. I'll take that as a compliment."

"Where are you from?"

"The Central Coast."

Not very definitive. That could be anywhere from Salinas to Santa Maria, a stretch of over two hundred miles. She'd lived there, too, a very long time ago.

But she didn't pry, just made conversation, a prelude to asking him to spend a few very mutually satisfying hours with her.

If he didn't prove to be a dickhead.

"So what *do* you do?"

"I'm a CEO for a medium-size manufacturing firm," he answered, using her earlier phrasing.

She sipped her drink, looking at him over the rim. "Hmmm, a CEO." She looked around at the fine accouterments of his hotel. "Your company must be doing very well."

"Yes." Not a trace of smugness or conceit, just confidence. He leaned forward, his gaze traveling over her face. He continued the obligatory getting-to-know-you small talk. "So, Ms. Controller, what do *you* want to do with your life?"

Easy answer. "I want to be a CFO." Before she turned forty. Only five short years away.

"At the same company?"

"Hopefully. But not necessarily. What about you?"

"I want to be Chairman of the Board."

"I like a man who knows what he wants."

"I like a woman who knows what *she* wants." A wealth of innuendo lurked beneath the words, smoldered in his hot eyes, simmered in his smile.

Justine sucked in a breath. She'd never get a better opening. Butterflies swarmed in her stomach, and beneath her skirt, she felt herself moisten.

And all the while Len watched her as if suddenly she'd become the prey and he the predator.

She'd bought the condoms. She'd shaved, lathered, scented and lotioned. Damn, he was so tempting. But she hadn't quite made up her mind about him yet. Just a little more conversation seemed necessary.

"I dearly love my career."

"What about family?"

"All my family's dead." She ran her finger around the rim of her glass as she wrapped her lips around the lie.

He stared at her with unreadable eyes, then murmured with an eye on her ring finger, "I'm sorry. What about kids, husband?"

She let out a puff of air. "I know men hate to hear this, but while a man can have a career and a family, a woman can't, not and do motherhood or a spouse justice."

"You're right, we hate to hear it. But we also know how true it is. I take it you're opting for the career."

His tone told her nothing of how he felt about the statement, about her. She wouldn't volunteer her reasons for the choice.

"My career's important." Nor was she ashamed of that fact.

"A CFO's a lofty goal," he agreed.

His gaze roamed her face. Heat rose to her cheeks.

She detected no censure from him at all.

"So, no marriage. What about a steady boyfriend?"

She shook her head. "If they don't have marriage on their minds, single men seem to prefer variety."

She'd soon find out if she did, too. With this man. Len was growing on her.

"Variety, yes, but that doesn't mean always having a different woman. The variety can be in the act itself, the creativity a woman and a man put into it."

He sipped at his drink. The slight smack of his lips drew her attention. She squeezed her thighs together for relief, but the action only made the ache worse.

How the hell had they gotten into this conversation? He wasn't simply growing on her, she'd made the choice. If she didn't ask him to bed soon, she'd simply melt on the bench seat listening to that voice.

He looked at her expectantly. Had he said something? Drowning in her own thoughts and his coffee-colored eyes, she hadn't heard. His glass sat on the table, and the heat of his hand jumped across the three inches that separated their fingers.

Holding his gaze, she said, "I'd like very much to test out my creativity with you."

The words fell into the deepest, darkest silence, the kind where all the voices fade, the laughter mutes—the moment between life and death, love and hate, yes and no.

He felt it, too, and drew it out until finally he exhaled.

"I thought you'd never ask."

Ah, perfect.

CHAPTER TWO

A decisive man, he reached into his back pocket, pulled out his wallet, threw some bills on the table.

"Wait, that was my turn."

He grabbed her hand and pulled Justine to her feet. "Next time. Right now, we don't have time to quibble over technicalities."

Two and a half glasses of wine, damp panties, and a need so strong that she felt dizzy standing next to him said he was right.

His apparent eagerness shot her own excitement level even higher.

The elevator was crowded. Too many bodies, too much perfume, people going up, people going down—oh, what a tempting thought.

They wedged themselves into a corner. His breath seduced her hair, her ear. His hands circled her hips, pulled her back into his undeniable erection. He rotated slightly against the seam of her butt. She wanted to scream.

If he didn't stop, she'd come—without even his hand up her skirt.

I can't believe I'm doing this. One thing to contemplate it, quite another to take the step.

He was a total stranger.

His fingers eased up the hem of her skirt until they found the heat of the bare skin of her thigh. She wanted to beg him to stop, or, better yet, beg him to finish her on the spot.

She bit her lip to hold back a moan. The only thing keeping her on her feet were his hands.

The elevator dinged to a stop, the cessation of movement disorienting. He pushed her lightly forward, through the remaining passengers and out into the hall.

Not even waiting for the final whoosh of the closing doors, he took her face in his hands and licked her lips. She turned it into a kiss, opening her mouth, tasting him. A needy moan escaped her throat. He sizzled like the soda he'd drunk, and she rose on her toes to wrap her arms around his neck.

She had to feel all of him, his firm chest, abdomen, and that oh-so-hard bulge in his jeans.

He heard the footsteps muffled by carpet before she did. Breathing hard, he tucked her beneath his arm and exited the elevator hall, passing a nattily dressed couple.

Two doors down, he stopped, fished in his pocket for a card key. He opened the door, then pulled her inside. In the short hall, with the lights off, the electric blaze of nighttime San Francisco softly illuminated the room through the sheer curtains.

He backed her up against the wall, eyes glittering in the semi-dark.

"Screw creativity, for now," he whispered against her lips. "I'm only interested in getting your panties off."

She laughed, half nerves, half insane desire. "Be my guest."

Nimble fingers slid up her thighs. Encountering her rounded cheeks, he cupped, squeezed, groaned, then moved on to her hi-cut thong. He pushed around the elastic, pulling her panties down, skimming her curls, her swollen lips, her clitoris, her thighs.

She wanted to scream, would have if he hadn't put his mouth on hers.

"Please," she murmured against his lips.

Her thong cascaded down her calves and caught on her shoe. She kicked it aside.

God, she wanted him inside. Her legs parted in anticipation. His fingers found her first. He buried two deep inside her, drew them out. Slowly. Endlessly. She thought she'd die.

He trailed the crease of her sex, fingertip edging across her clitoris. She was so hot, so ready, it took only that single touch.

She did scream this time, put her head back against the wall and cried out as the delicious orgasmic shudders went on and on. Her body sucked at his fingers, took everything he had until she would have collapsed but for his arms around her.

She'd barely caught her breath when his hands skimmed up beneath her shirt, drawing the material over her head. He tossed it aside, then covered her breasts with his palms. A slight tremor passed through him.

"God. I haven't felt like this in …" He licked the seam of her lips. "Not in a long time."

The tone made her shiver in the air-conditioned room. Then he popped the front snap of her bra and threw that aside, too.

Warm hands covered her hardened nipples. She arched into his touch and purred as he rolled her nipples between thumb and forefinger. She reached behind and unzipped her skirt. He pushed it past her hips, and she stepped out. Now, she wore only her high heels.

He sucked in a breath, moved back. His gaze was everywhere, touching her, heating her.

"A shower," he murmured. "We need a shower, or I'm not going to last." He cupped her chin in one hand. "And I want this to last."

He pulled her into the bathroom, flipped on the light. Her heels clicked on the tile floor. In the mirror, his hands caressed her breasts as he bent and nipped her neck. Her nudity should have made her vulnerable, but his rock-hard cock at the base of her spine expunged any embarrassment. Her skin flushed. Her eyes shone. Her lips were wet and full.

She loved the picture they made in the mirror, watching as he removed his clothes, his body half-hidden behind her. He nudged the back of her knee with his, and she stepped out of her shoes. Then he tugged her beneath the hot stinging spray, setting her before him so the water pounded her belly.

It was unbelievably erotic. He smoothed soap over her body, slid over her breasts, then slipped down between her legs. She wanted to beg him to make her come again.

Instead, Justine took the soap and turned. Oh. He was beautiful. Strong chest, hard abdomen, and … way more than a mouthful. Yep, the promise in those tight jeans was right on. She massaged lather onto his cock, around his balls.

"Jesus, maybe the shower wasn't a good idea. I'm supposed to be holding out here."

"I don't want you to hold out."

Then she went to her knees, moved her shoulder aside to let the soap wash down the drain, and took him in her mouth.

His hands fisted in her wet hair. Water pummeled the back of her head. She closed her eyes as it rained down on her while she tasted the saltiness of him. The scent of soap and sex filled her.

"Justine, wait." He hauled her to her feet, slammed the water off, then pushed aside the shower curtain, seeking a towel. "When I come the first time, I want to be inside you."

She smiled, loving the power. "Then get inside me."

They stepped out. She slipped on the watery floor. His hands steadied, then lifted her to the cold tile counter. She relished the feel of it against her overheated flesh.

"Shit, I don't have a condom."

"My purse," she told him without a flutter of embarrassment.

He returned with her bag. After she'd made the purchase, she'd simply opened the box and dumped the contents into her purse. Now she pulled out a line of three.

Separating a packet, he ripped the foil and rolled on the condom.

There was something about watching a man touch himself.

He spread her legs, rubbed his finger across her clitoris. Then, with a groan, he was inside. She let her head fall back, sighing, and gripped his shoulders as he began to move.

"Christ, you're tight."

"And you're huge."

He chuckled, eyes shut. "Don't make me laugh right now."

"Afraid you'll lose it?"

He opened his eyes, stared hard, his hips flush against her. "I'm afraid I might fuck you right into the mirror."

She pulled her legs up, wrapped them around his waist and locked her feet behind him. Shower steam coated her flesh. Her fingers slipped on his arms.

"Fuck away."

She didn't last long beneath the onslaught. When she came the second time, she bit down on his shoulder.

When he came, she bit him again.

~

He took her beneath the bedclothes, on the carpet, in the chair, on the desk. Creativity abounded. By midnight, she was boneless and sleepy and satisfied beyond her wildest fantasies.

Len. She didn't know his last name; he didn't know hers. But she relished the feel of his arms enveloping her, the solid heat of his body at her back. Justine stretched, put her arms over her head, squirmed under the covers next to him. Perfect.

His arm snaked around her waist and pulled her back against him. He nuzzled her neck, his chin pleasantly rough with beard shadow. He was hard, *again*. Even after he'd given her five hours of the best sex she'd ever had.

Good thing she'd bought the condom multi-pak.

But like Cinderella … "It's late, I have to go."

He hesitated a moment, his hand squeezing her breast. "I'll get dressed and walk you down. Do you need a cab or is your car parked nearby?"

The practical side of her appreciated the offer; the needy side wondered why he didn't ask her to stay the night. Oh yeah, it really was time to leave.

"A cab. Thanks."

She found her panties by the door, her skirt next to them, her shirt and bra on the bed. Her shoes, where were they? Ah, the bathroom floor. They'd been the last thing to come off.

She smoothed her hair in the mirror, freshened her lipstick and smiled at the stars in her eyes.

The experiment had worked splendidly. She didn't intend to indulge herself often. But, a career woman still had needs. Once a quarter, perhaps, after the audit review.

Len was dressed when she came out of the bathroom. With his back to her, he pulled on a black leather jacket, then grabbed something from the desk and stuck it in his inside pocket.

Out in the hallway, he tucked her beneath his arm, fingers burrowing under her hair to stroke her neck. More than sexual satiation, the lassitude stealing through her came from the warmth of his arm around her. An almost scary contentment. She couldn't afford to like this man too much.

Besides, he'd said he was going home tomorrow—today— back to the Central Coast. True, it was only a matter of hours away by car ... but she wouldn't ask to see him again.

The elevator was empty. He pressed his lips lightly to hers, the act reflected in the mirrored walls surrounding them. They didn't look like a couple who had met six hours ago. She almost wished for words to douse this too-perfect afterglow.

The lobby, though far from full, resounded with tempered voices and muted footsteps. The doorman smiled as if he remembered them. A line of yellow cabs rumbled curbside. Len followed her down the steps, stopped her with a touch to her elbow.

He reached inside his jacket and pulled out an envelope. "This is for you."

A strange lightness weakened her legs, made her dizzy. "I didn't do this for money."

His mouth lifted in a half smile. "It's not money. It's a letter."

He handed it over.

Her name was written on the front, the handwriting vaguely familiar. Her heart started to pound and she looked up at Len, dreading whatever he had to say.

His eyes turned inscrutable. "It's from your 'dead' father."

The parchment seemed to burn her fingertips.

"I'm your father's CEO," he went on. "My mother married him last year. Guess that makes you my sister."

The man shot her a killer smile. "But I sure as hell don't think I'm feeling the slightest bit brotherly. Not after that exquisite fuck."

CHAPTER THREE

Len Falconer had been prepared to tolerate her, because his stepfather, Walter Jarreau, wanted his daughter to come home.

He hadn't been prepared to fall head-first into lust with her.

He felt only the slightest qualm about his actions. She'd walked out on her family obligations fifteen years ago, and she hadn't spoken to her father since. She harbored no sense of loyalty, therefore, he harbored no need to coddle her feelings.

Her blue eyes flared. Walter's letter crumpled in her fingers. Her jaw tensed, tremors rippled across her cheeks. Her right hand fisted, then flexed, as if she'd like to slap the hell out of him. Len's gaze rose to her lush lips shimmering with crimson gloss.

"Maybe I should paraphrase the letter for you." He didn't wait for her answer. "Your father had a heart attack last week."

Emotions played over her face. Her brow furrowed. Her lips tightened. But the remorse he searched for wasn't there. He doubted the woman regretted her treachery, either now or fifteen years ago.

But Walter wanted her back. And Len would do whatever was necessary to get what the old man needed. Walter Jarreau was family now. "He wants you to come home."

"So he sent you to butter me up?"

"The buttering up was my idea." Allowing one corner of his mouth to lift, he smiled. "But only after you offered so sweetly."

"You dickhead."

He supposed, looking at it from her perspective, that he deserved the epithet. He hadn't intended to follow her from her apartment. His original plan had been to confront her right away. But, mesmerized by those endless legs of hers, he'd allowed her to jump into a cab. He followed, then pursued her into the restaurant to see who she met, to gauge any competition he'd encounter on Walter's behalf.

But hell, by the time she sipped the cocktail he'd sent her, he was hooked. And that hadn't bothered him one bit.

"I'll pick you up at nine o'clock tomorrow morning and drive you home." He pointedly looked at his watch. "I mean, *this* morning."

"So you can make sure I go?"

"Yes." After all, she'd turned her back on her father before; he presumed she'd require pressure to go back now. Then again, maybe she'd think about the sizable inheritance she stood to gain by reconciling with her father.

"You don't know where I live."

"I know everything there is to know about you, Miss Jarreau."

Her expression was still, not a muscle flinched. Only the fire deep in her sky blue eyes revealed her rage.

"You know *nothing* about me." Then she balled the letter in her hand and stepped towards the first cab in line. Like a shadow, the doorman was there to hold the back passenger side open for her.

"Aren't you even interested in how he's doing?"

She switched her purse to her other hand, almost hugging it to her luscious breasts. Fingertips on the cab door, she stopped, waited, but said nothing.

Len moved closer. "He's home from the hospital. But his doctor isn't sounding optimistic enough for me. And he certainly can't keep going at the pace he was."

Her eyes glittered in the city lights. "So I guess you'll get to be Chairman of the Board PDQ, won't you?"

He'd been CEO for three years. Wanting the chairmanship wasn't a question of ousting her father. He ignored the slam.

But the delectable Ms. Jarreau didn't wait for his answer. She slammed the car door and leaned forward to give directions to the cabbie.

He'd sworn to Walter that he'd get her to come home. He'd sworn to himself that he'd accept her as part of the family despite what she'd done to her father. Forgiveness was Walter's alone to give.

Run-away daughter, stepsister, ball-busting executive, Len had put Justine in all sorts of convenient categories when he'd planned this short jaunt. But he hadn't expected that driving need to make love to her. Nor later, the urge to ask her to spend the rest of the night. He'd resisted that insane impulse.

But that didn't stop him from wanting her in his bed again. And again.

~

Justine's eyes were bleary from lack of sleep, but her mind hummed and her fingers trembled on the phone from the effects of two strong cups of coffee.

"I'm sorry to bother you so early on a Saturday, Mr. Freidman."

"Is everything all right with the audit, Justine?"

In the semi-casual atmosphere honed in Silicon Valley, her boss's required use of Mister was demanded rather than earned. The show of respect was not something he gave in return.

"The work papers are ready and waiting in the conference room I've assigned the auditors. However, I wanted to let you know that I'd be out of town for a little while. My father's very ill. I hope to be back by—"

"What's wrong with him?"

She stuck the phone receiver between her shoulder and ear, then smoothed her father's now well-read, semi-crumpled letter on the kitchen table.

"He's had a heart attack."

Freidman cleared his throat. "Oftentimes indigestion can be misconstrued as a heart attack."

God. The inane, unsympathetic, even idiotic, comment was just like him. She held her breath in an attempt to control her temper. She was sure the audible exhale that followed carried across the phone line. "I'm afraid it's *very* serious, Mr. Freidman."

The letter begged her come. To attend her father's deathbed. Her eyes stung. Dammit, she would not start crying on the phone with Mr. Freidman.

And she would not beg for the time off. "As I started to say, I hope to be there for the beginning of the audit on Monday, however—"

Again, he cut her off. "I don't recall you mentioning your family. How long has it been since you've seen your father?"

Guilt squeezed her heart. The wounds from the long ago battle throbbed as if they were still fresh. "Fifteen years."

"Well, then, you see."

See? See what?

What she *saw* was that Mr. Freidman had the sensitivity of a man grown in a test tube. "My father may be dying."

And she'd let pride stand in the way of calling him. She'd wanted him to do the contacting since he'd done the disowning.

But my God, he'd gotten *married* without even telling her.

"Take the weekend. I'm sure everything will be fine. I'll expect you on Monday. Goodbye, my dear."

She held the receiver away from her ear, stared at it, the dial tone buzzing loudly in the quiet of her apartment.

"Bite me," she whispered aloud, then thought immediately of Len and those innumerable love bites he'd given her last night.

Damn him for giving her the letter instead of breaking the news ... gently.

She rose from the table, stomped to the kitchen sink and slammed down her empty coffee mug. A chip of ceramic flew off the bottom.

And damn him for making her break things. CEO of a medium-sized manufacturing firm, my ass. He was CEO of Jarreau Wineries, her father's family-bred, family-owned, family-run company. How the hell did Len Falconer fit into it, a man who considered wine-making synonymous with "manufacturing?" Bastard.

Her bag was packed with the essentials; she was ready to leave an hour and a half before Len said he'd be by to pick her up. She wouldn't be waiting with bated breath for that to happen. Rounding the kitchen door, she turned down the short hallway for one last trip to the bathroom.

And toppled over her suitcase.

"Dammit, dammit, dammit."

The tears she'd kept at bay with Mr. Freidman blurred her vision. Her toe throbbed. And her anger with Len Falconer blew out of control. Climbing to her feet, she glared at the wavering image of her suitcase, then drew back her undamaged foot and kicked it.

"That's for having sex with me."

She kicked it again and sent it scudding across the carpet into the small foyer.

"That's for making me *like* having your arms around me."

Another vicious punt careened the offending bag into the front door with a thud.

"And that's for being my goddamn stepbrother."

She swiped at her damp cheeks and sniffed. God, that felt good, despite the pulsing of her injured foot. She was almost sorry now that she hadn't given in to the urge to belt him last night. That would have felt extremely good, too.

The door shook with a hard knock.

Oh shit. Please God, don't let it be him.

"Justine, are you all right in there?"

God was definitely not paying attention to her this morning.

She glanced in the foyer mirror. Blood-shot, red-rimmed eyes stared back. Her nose glowed like Rudolph's. But at least her mascara hadn't run. Still, if she opened the door, Len would know she'd been crying.

"Justine?"

But if she didn't open the door, he'd probably beat it down. Not good for her neighborly image at 7:30 in the morning.

Screw it! What the hell did she care if he thought she'd been crying anyway? Scooting the suitcase back, she undid the deadbolt, removed the chain and yanked on the door handle.

"I am not driving down to Templeton with you." She wanted her own car at her disposal when she went home. Being marooned in Templeton was more than she could contemplate without going crazy. Besides, four hours trapped in a vehicle with Len was completely out of the question.

Especially with his dark hair still wet from a recent shower and a teal polo shirt accentuating a devastating set of pectorals. How could the mere scent of shampoo and toothpaste touch off that electric current suddenly arcing through her body?

"That's fine. I don't mind following you." He looked down at her hips encased in tight denim. "In fact, I'll relish the view."

The man might be gorgeous, but he was still an ass.

"What *we* did last night has nothing to do with my father's heart attack. Just because you used sex to get me to do what you wanted will not stop me from seeing my father. But I will not drive down with you, and I will not let you control my every move."

He quirked an eyebrow. "Does that mean a quickie before we leave is out of the question?"

CHAPTER FOUR

Her hands fisted at her sides. She pursed her succulent lips and narrowed stormy eyes. Her reddened, puffy lower lids indicated she'd been crying, but the woman wasn't about to let that stop her from going to battle.

God, she was magnificent. He wanted his tongue down her throat, his hands on her breasts, and his cock deep inside her.

That wasn't quite politic at the moment.

Len fully admitted he'd been a dickhead last night. Mixing business and pleasure had never been his intention. At least not until he'd seen her. Nor had he'd used sex as a tool to manipulate her. He'd simply wanted her. He wanted her now. His actions, however, might have botched the whole plan. Antagonizing Justine wasn't going to bring her home permanently. So he'd make nice, apologize.

If that didn't work, he'd confirm that her father would reinstate her in the will if she returned for good.

He raised both hands in surrender. "Sorry. Bad joke. And about last night …"

She waited, the tempest in her eyes showing no signs of dissipating.

"My actions last evening were not particularly … well thought-out," he said.

He hadn't been thinking at all. And if he kept staring at her breasts outlined in that stretchy, snug sweater, remembering the texture of her nipples on his tongue, he'd cease thinking again and bury himself inside her right here in the front hall.

Of course, there were the snug jeans hugging her sweet ass, too. A helluva lot of distractions about the woman.

"Not well thought-out," she repeated with an edge of sarcasm.

"Perhaps reprehensible would be a better description?"

"Not vile enough." But the stormy glint began to abate.

"How about dickhead? Asshole?"

"Scummy."

Could he actually get her to smile? The idea appealed for reasons that had nothing to do with her father. "Fucked?"

"Yeah. Totally." Her lips twitched with a near smile.

Enticing shades of the woman he'd made love to last night slipped through. The air around them heated. The sudden silence settled like the warm brush of flesh against flesh. Christ, if they stayed in her small foyer much longer, with the scent of almond shampoo or lotion or whatever the hell it was teasing his senses, he wouldn't be responsible.

He stepped around her to grab her suitcase. "I'll carry it down to the car for you."

Her icy Jarreau demeanor snapped back into place. "I said I'm driving myself. I have to be back for work on Monday."

All the more reason that she should drive with him, so he could disabuse her of that idea right away. With four hours on a long highway, he was sure he could melt the glacier.

Ah hell, why not the admit the truth to himself. He just plain wanted her with him.

"No," she said.

Obviously, his thoughts were written on his face, though he couldn't fathom how the hell that had happened. He was known for his enigmatic expressions. He could bluff his way to the winner's pot with nothing but a pair of deuces.

But not with Justine. He decided to let her win this one. "I meant I'd take it down to *your* car."

"I'm not ready. You don't need to wait for me."

"I don't mind."

She cocked a hip and jammed a hand on it. "Don't bother."

Shit. The war was starting all over again.

~

She'd almost succumbed. Almost forgotten why she hated his guts. Almost begged him to let her blow him in his car, speeding along the highway at a hundred miles an hour, racing towards climax. Luckily she'd crashed into the brick wall of his high-handedness before she'd totally lost her mind and agreed to get in his car.

They made a pit stop at a fast food place in Gilroy, then again in King City. She'd only needed to use the bathroom and down a cool cup of water, and she'd managed quite successfully to ignore him.

Or at least to pretend she was ignoring him.

Of course, watching the muscles of his neck work as he chugged his own drink made her heart pound and turned her legs boneless.

She had to swallow another eight ounces just to wet her parched throat. Not that it had worked completely.

Thank God, they were almost to Templeton. Her hometown was on the Central Coast. Outside of California, where Napa was the equivalent of "wine country," it was ignored that in the south, along the coast and into the valley, stretched mile after mile of vineyards.

She'd called this place home until she was twenty.

Justine's hands started to tremble on the wheel of her Toyota Camry.

Home. She hadn't been home in fifteen years. She hadn't heard her father's voice. She hadn't thrown her arms around his bulk nor luxuriated in the crush of one of his great big, all-consuming bear hugs. She hadn't laughed with him until she cried. She hadn't sat in front of a warm fire on a cold night in the quiet of the library, her father's soft snore a soothing balm after a long day. She hadn't done any of those things. But, she also hadn't had to storm from the house after he'd beaten her goals to pulp. She hadn't lost yet another of their bitter arguments. She'd been master of her own future.

Yet she had lost something. She'd lost her sense of belonging. Her sense of home.

Gravel spit from beneath the tires as she turned into the long lane. Rhododendron bushes in full bloom lined the drive, lush reds, sweetheart pinks, pristine whites. The vibrant lawn beyond the hedge flourished despite the low rainfall much of California had received this year.

She came to a stop at the bottom of flagstone steps fronting the ornate, century-old manor house. It resembled something out of the French countryside, stately, manicured, a trifle sterile. As a child, even as a teenager, she'd seldom used the front entrance, preferring the back door through the kitchen.

In the rearview mirror she watched Len pull in behind her in his sparkling white Jaguar XK-8. Climbing from the low-slung sports car with elegant ease, he approached her door, putting his hand out, then pulling it back.

She relished the sense of having him on the run. She had something he wanted—not her body, but her seeming importance to her father—and Len was actually afraid of screwing it all up. Wonderful.

She opened her own door and stepped out, ankle boots crunching on gravel. He was close. He was tall. His woodsy cologne smelled too damn good. Last night, she hadn't noticed the height difference quite so much in her four-inch spikes. She definitely hadn't noticed it when he had her on the countertop or stretched out on the bed beneath him. Looking up at him stole some of her advantage.

"I'd like to see my father right away."

"I'm sure he's waiting. Let me have your keys, and I'll tell Roberts to take your suitcase upstairs to your room."

He held out his hand. She stared at the long life-line bisecting his palm. The thought of relinquishing her keys to him raised goose bumps along her arms. But these weren't medieval times where the dark knight locked the damsel in the tower until she yielded to him.

Although Len Falconer did strike her as a throwback to earlier days, a man who took instead of asked, who conquered instead of wooed.

But, dammit, she didn't want wooing. Justine allowed her key ring to drop into his open palm.

"I'll go up."

He fell into step beside her as she climbed the flagstones. "I'll show you the way."

"I *know* the way."

He chuckled softly, sending air currents to caress her ear. "Are you going to fight me every step?"

"You aren't worth the bother."

She felt his hand on her elbow like a branding iron. "Oh, I bother you, sweetheart. And we both know it."

Then the door was flung open, and a slim, dark-haired woman threw herself into Len's arms.

CHAPTER FIVE

"Thank God, you're home."

Len pried his mother's arms from around his neck and gently urged her back so that he could look down at her face.

His pulse raced as a shot of adrenaline surged through his veins. "Is he all right?"

"Roman just left."

Walter's doctor. "And?"

"The same. Nothing worse."

Len didn't realize he'd been holding his breath until it seemed to rush out of his lungs in one long, relieved sigh.

He looked more closely at his mother. Worry lines creased her forehead, strain flattened her lips, and gray streaked her auburn hair. She showed every minute of her sixty years. A week ago, he wouldn't have said she looked over fifty.

She glanced past his shoulder.

Draping his arm about her, he turned. "Mom, I want you to meet Justine."

"I can't believe you're finally here." She pushed from his embrace to rush the two steps down to Justine's side. "I'm

Naomi." She paused, her arms halfway outstretched for a hug. "Your stepmother."

Justine swallowed, parted her lips, then closed them again. Like an electric storm, tension crackled in the air. She stared. Then her gaze flicked to his, her blue eyes enormous and uncertain.

His mother's arms fell back to her side. In the long silence, Len was glad he couldn't see his mother's face. She'd had high hopes. Family reunion. Smiles, happy faces, hugs and laughter. Everything to help take her mind off Walter's life and death struggle.

Justine wasn't giving his mother any of those things.

"Perhaps you'd like to see your father now," his mother offered tentatively.

Justine still didn't move, didn't offer a word. But her brow furrowed suddenly, and a shudder traveled across her shoulders.

Say something, he wanted to shout at her. *Do something*. He couldn't stand his mother's disappointment.

"This must all be a terrible shock to you." His mother, ever the nurturer, laid a hand on Justine's arm. "A whole new family to get to know, your father's illness."

"Yes. It's been … " Justine bit her lip. "Hard."

She glanced his way. Moisture shimmered on her eyelashes. Purple shadows lurked beneath her eyes. A sleepless night? He hadn't thought to ask how she felt about the entire situation, even with the evidence of those red-rimmed eyes this morning. He hadn't considered that she had any emotions beyond avarice or anger.

In his quest to reach this moment, he hadn't cared enough to ask what the hell Justine felt.

His mother had picked up on her state immediately.

"Perhaps a cup of tea first," she suggested.

Justine drew a deep breath; the intake of oxygen seemed to revive her. "Thank you, but no. I'd really like to see my father first." She flashed Len a steely-eyed glance. "Len really didn't tell me much about his condition."

He'd told her everything he knew, though he'd kept his fears to himself.

The woman who'd stood in her small foyer, matching him glare for glare, was back. He liked her better. Rather, he understood her better, knew how to deal with her. An emotional Justine was beyond his grasp.

He had enough to deal with, worrying about Walter, his mother and the rest of his family.

~

Naomi was Justine's approximate size and height, her hair shades lighter than Len's. But the eyes, the same expressive brown, they were the clue these two were mother and son.

She hadn't expected her stepmother to be so young. Naomi couldn't be more than sixty. Her father was now—her stomach clenched—seventy-five. Nor had she expected the kindness brimming in the woman's eyes, a kindness that almost had tears welling in her own.

The question hit home again. How could her father get married without even calling her? Without even sending a letter? Pain throbbed like a sharp stick wedged between her ribs.

All right, maybe if she'd called a few times or sent a letter or even checked the society pages of a local newspaper ... but then she'd had her pride, just as her father had. She was his daughter after all.

Len at her side, Justine followed the trim figure of her new stepmother along the familiar upstairs hallway.

The carpet was new, a rich, deep burgundy, accenting the dark paneling that still covered the walls. Flowers overflowed vases on two long trestle tables, their perfume scenting the air.

She clenched her trembling hands at her sides. A lump constricted her throat. Her head demanded she see her father for herself. Her heart was terrified of what she'd find.

Naomi stopped at the closed door of her father's room, the same room he'd occupied all her life. Naomi knocked softly, then opened the door.

"She's here," she called lightly and entered.

Justine wanted to run. She wanted to beg Naomi to let her see her father alone. She loathed the idea of an audience, especially Len, scrutinizing her every word and action. Instead, she studiously avoided Len's penetrating gaze and followed her stepmother into the room.

Through the drawn velvet curtains, a sliver of afternoon sunlight managed to streak across the Persian carpet. A bedside lamp glowed, but didn't fully penetrate the shadows beneath the big canopy. She had a vague impression of piled pillows, a dark figure reclining against them.

Her father, a bear of a man when she'd left, seemed dwarfed by the massive bed he lay in.

Naomi's warm, insistent hand propelled her forward. The child in her wanted to dig in her heels. Then suddenly, she stood beside her father.

"Justine."

Once, his voice would have filled the quiet with a boom. Now, it was low, raspy, weak. His cheeks had sunk; his chin was grizzled. Loose flesh hung at his throat.

"Thank God, you came."

"You've lost weight."

She didn't mean to say it, should have said hello, I love you, I missed you. Something, anything. But all she could see was the once-vital, now-emaciated body lying on that bed.

"Oh, I've had him on a healthy diet, even before …" Naomi's words trailed off. "No red meat. Lots of vegetables and fiber."

Justine's father grimaced, and she saw a glimpse of his former self. "She's trying to starve me."

"She's trying to take care of you, Walter. You should listen to her," Len said, concerned reproach lacing his tone.

He might be several unpleasant things, but Len Falconer was protective of his mother. Justine had seen that in the fierce hug he'd given her upon their arrival, the worry frown marring his forehead.

She also had to admit that Len cared for her father.

Walter might have lost his daughter, but he'd managed to surround himself with people who seemed to care about him. He had not been alone those fifteen long years.

Unlike Justine.

Guilt dampened the sudden bitterness. He was ill, possibly dying. Whatever stood between them no longer mattered.

She reached for his hand amidst the rumpled bedclothes. "Are you all right?" He looked terrible, but she wanted to pretend.

He cleared his throat with a phlegmy cough, his gaze on the canopy above. "I'll be fine."

"You look like crap," Len barked. "And you'll stay in bed until Roman says you're fit."

Even Justine recognized the fear in Len's command.

Her father gave a weak smile. "He just loves this opportunity to boss me around."

The affection was obvious. She pursed her lips to keep her emotions inside. She wasn't proud of the fact that she was jealous. It was unbecoming. Selfish. Unwarranted.

Except that it was *her* father lying there, not Len's, and Justine felt like the outsider here.

"What does the doctor say?" She was glad for the apparent calm in her voice.

Her father looked past her to Naomi, and something indefinable passed between them. Justine couldn't decide if it was grief, worry, or thankfulness. Perhaps it was all of those things.

Then Naomi's eyes misted, and she quickly took his hand, squeezing. "Roman says we were lucky, sweetheart. So let's not press that luck today, okay? Maybe you should rest now."

"Yes, yes, I need to rest," he muttered, then he pierced Justine with his gaze. "You won't leave, though, will you?"

"I'm not going anywhere, Dad. We'll talk more when you wake up."

She bent to kiss his cheek, her lips brushing the papery flesh. He smelled ... medicinal. Old. The scent impacted her viscerally, cramping her belly.

Her eyes suddenly burned with the need to cry. She held her breath to blot out the odor surrounding him. Her head swam. God, she needed to get out. Away.

She stepped back, bumped up against Len, and felt her knees begin to buckle. Only Len's strong grip on her arms kept her upright, his touch strangely comforting despite the angry words that had occurred between them.

"We'll see you later, Walter, after dinner." Len's words puffed against her hair as he drew her backwards, enveloping her with his warmth.

Her father held out a hand before it dropped weakly back to the bed. "Promise?"

"Of course, I promise," she answered, amazed at the steady tone even as she wanted to collapse on the bed beside him. Her father had never begged for anything in his life.

God, how close was he to leaving her forever?

CHAPTER SIX

"All right, tell me what the doctor really said. Walter looks and sounds a helluva lot worse than when I left yesterday."

His mother put a finger to her lips and signaled both him and Justine to follow her down the hall. She stopped at the top of the stairs, one hand on the newel post.

Facing away from them and staring down into the front entry, she said, "He needs rest. That's all."

Len didn't let it go. His mother was hiding something, and the idea that it was a turn for the worse in Walter's health twisted knots in his gut.

"Mother, what are you not telling me?"

She ran a hand through her hair, then let it fall stiffly back to her side. "Roman didn't say anything else. I swear."

Len put a gentle hand on her arm and tugged her around to face him. "You're not lying about his condition, are you?"

She gasped, somewhat overly dramatic. "Why would I lie to you? About something like that?"

He shook his head. "I don't know. But I get the feeling you're hiding something."

And dammit, it scared him.

She gave him a direct look then. "I swear to you, Len, Roman only said that Walter needed rest. He had a close call. You know that." Then she muscled him aside. "Goodness, look what you've done to Justine."

Shit. Justine stood back by the wall, one hand across her stomach, her knees slightly bent.

"Honey, are you all right?" His mother smoothed hair back from Justine's forehead.

Christ, he'd forgotten about her in his need for answers. Even though he couldn't deny her disturbing reaction in Walter's room. He could almost believe she cared. He had the sudden, irresistible urge to shove his mother away, to once more give Justine the comfort of his body.

Justine straightened. "Fine. I'm just tired."

His formidable mother scowled. "Did you feed this girl, Leonard?"

"She didn't want to eat." His wasn't sure why the use of his full name reduced him to childhood.

"Well, she looks like she's going to faint from hunger."

"I'll take care of her."

Justine merely stared at them both. His hands ached to touch her.

"Dear, why don't you freshen up? Mrs. Danaher is fixing us an early dinner anyway, thinking you might be exhausted. The children will be home soon, and they'll be hungry, too."

"The children?" Justine murmured.

"Darla and Brian. My daughter. My other son."

Justine started to slip down the wall.

"Leonard, didn't you tell her?"

He grabbed her before she went all the way down and picked her up, holding her to his chest. Her body heat seeped into his marrow.

"It slipped my mind," he told his mother.

"Leonard Falconer, you are an ass."

Who else had called him that recently, this morning, in fact? Justine and his mother were going to get along famously.

Now all he had to do was take care of his stepfather's needs by making sure Justine didn't leave again.

~

"I did *not* faint," Justine hissed.

She'd heard his mother's voice just fine. She'd even relished the strength of his arms as he'd carried her to her room. She simply hadn't felt like replying at the time. And she didn't feel like rehashing it all now.

Especially when they were on their way down to dinner to meet the rest of his family.

The rest of *her* family.

The one the bastard hadn't even told her about, bastard being a technical term and not a slur on his sweet mother.

Len put a solicitous hand to her elbow as they descended the stairs. "You were out cold when I laid you on the bed."

Her lip curled involuntarily. "Isn't that how you prefer your women? Out cold so they can't talk back?"

He laughed, not a bit perturbed. "They might not be able to talk back," he leaned down to whisper against her ear. "But they also can't lick me, kiss me, or suck me the way you did."

"You're disgusting."

But a shiver of awareness tingled down to her fingertips. And she hated it. She hated, too, that he'd made her feel protected and comforted in her father's room.

God, her father. How could she be feeling anything remotely sexual when her father lay alone, and possibly dying, upstairs in his room? And how could she have allowed that momentary flicker of envy at the obvious closeness he shared with his new family? No matter what her father had done fifteen years ago, those feelings were not right under the circumstances.

She squashed her irritation with Len.

They entered the dining room together. Naomi was already seated at the end nearest the kitchen. "Dear, are you feeling better?"

"Fine, thank you," she replied as Len pulled out a chair for her.

"You look rested. Much better."

"I do feel better." The hour had made a world of difference. She shook out her napkin and draped it over her lap.

Len took her father's place at the head of the table.

Justine stifled her outrage. This was no longer her home. Seating arrangements weren't her business.

"Where are ..." Damn, she couldn't remember the children's names. She wondered how much younger they were than Len. Perhaps his mother had had a marriage in between Walter Jarreau and Len's father, and produced a whole new set of offspring.

"Darla and Brian? They'll be down soon."

Just as Naomi spoke, booted heels sounded on the parquet flooring of the front hall and two twenty-something whirling dervishes burst into the dining room. They skidded to a stop just behind Len.

God, they were twins. Or as close as you could get without being the same sex. And they were not *children*. Darla's nut-brown hair fell past her shoulders. Brian's was just short of a buzz cut. They both sported jeans and short-sleeved t-shirts. Darla was the one wearing the boots. The resemblance to Len, dark hair, brown eyes, same strong facial lines, was remarkable.

They spoke together, their voices mingling in sing-song.

"Hey, you must be Justine."

"Walter's told us tons about you."

Her father talked about her. A lot. Her heart twisted. Len watched her intently.

She gave him no visible reaction. "Nice to meet you."

Naomi rang a small bell at the side of her plate. The twins sat, and moments later, the swing door flapped open and a woman, presumably Mrs. Danaher, entered carrying a tureen.

"There you go. Split pea," she said as she placed it at Naomi's right and exited.

That was the extent of the formality.

"I hate split pea," Darla said.

"Me, too," Brian echoed.

"Well, I like it," Naomi said, unconcerned, glancing in Justine's direction.

The soup was Justine's favorite. Her mother's specialty. Naomi ladled a healthy portion into her dish and passed the rest on. The children passed the bowl to Len without taking any.

He filled his, watching Justine the whole time without losing a drop. They'd planned the menu around her. At least, Naomi had planned it with Len's approval.

"How long are you staying?" Darla's short, unadorned nails tinkled against the china.

"That depends on how well my father does."

She took the soup tureen from Len, her fingers brushing his with a crackle of electricity. She ignored it.

"He's going to be fine, you know." Brian took a deep breath after the declaration, almost as if willing himself to believe it.

"I know," she answered, then bent to her soup.

Darla, on her side of the table, seemed to be bursting with the enthusiasm and energy of a typical twenty-five year old. "I got the email from Knudsen Design of the first mockup."

Len glanced first at Justine, then raised a brow as if questioning Darla.

"The new label's gorgeous, Len. You're going to love it." She turned to Justine, including her. "Do you want to see it after dinner?"

At her end of the table, Naomi laced her fingers and cracked her knuckles.

Darla stared blankly. "That's not good for your hands, Mom. Causes arthritis." She turned back to Len. "Knudsen used the hooded falcon. It's so cool."

Justine's soup congealed in her stomach. New label? With a falcon?

Len gave her a saccharine-sweet smile. "We've been experimenting with some varietal changes in the vineyards. Darla here works in Marketing. She's coming up with a separate label for the venture. Brian's in Operations."

"You all work for Jarreau Wineries?" She tried to control the furious pace of her pulse.

"I don't," Naomi bleated.

And they had a new label. Featuring a falcon. Falconer? Duh. What next? Were they going to change the name to Falconer Wineries? She bit her lip.

Marketing, operations, new ventures. God, he talked about it all as if they were manufacturing Silicon Valley widgets instead of wine. Wine wasn't a mere "product" to be sold. Winemaking was an art form. The man didn't have a clue. So how could he run Jarreau's?

"Mrs. Danaher, we're ready for the roast beef and Yorkshires," Naomi called out, not bothering with the bell or waiting for the soup bowls to be emptied.

Roast beef and Yorkshire Pudding. Another of her favorites and her mother's specialties.

"Is Len going to take you to the winery and the vineyards?" Brian wanted to know. He puffed out his chest. "I'll take you through the plant."

She let out a shaky breath while her face heated beneath Len's scrutiny.

She knew what she wanted to blurt out. She'd practically grown up in the damn winery and in her father's vineyards, and the absolute last thing she wanted was a tour that would forcibly bring home the years she'd missed. The *life* she'd missed out on.

Still, simple politeness and Brian's obvious pride dictated her answer. "I'd like that."

But the bitter thoughts simmered inside her.

She'd grown up wanting that winery, wanting to run it the way her father had, wanting to put her own unique stamp on it. Create her own new labels, experiment with different grape varieties, make the decisions herself that would follow into future generations.

She'd have put her soul into Jarreau Wineries if her father had given her a chance. Wine was in her blood.

But he hadn't believed a woman could manage it. Now *she* accounted for fricking widgets at a damn Silicon Valley conglomerate with an asshole for a CFO.

Is this what her father had envisioned when he'd said *she'd* never be CEO of Jarreau, that they'd lose everything to a bunch of interlopers? Is this why he took her heritage away, why he cut her loose halfway through college?

She didn't realize she'd been holding her breath until her vision spotted. Then, she felt their eyes on her. Naomi worried; Darla and Brian confused. And Len, not sympathetic, something closer to acknowledgment.

It wasn't fair to blame them for the fact that her father had never believed in her—with the final affront being that her father had actually sanctioned a *female* member of the family working at the so-called "plant," even if it was just in Marketing. But that wasn't their fault either. She could feel their genuine concern. They were all just too damn nice, too damn caring. At least three-quarters of them.

But they were still taking over *her* family heritage.

"Len, why don't you pour Justine a glass of wine?" Naomi prompted.

Falconer wine? Oh, no, she couldn't stand it.

"I'm sorry, really sorry. I'm afraid I haven't recovered as well as I thought. I think I need to lie down again. If my father should wake up and want to see me—"

"I'll get you immediately, dear," Naomi assured her. "But I think he'll sleep through the evening. He did get a little overexcited when we knew you were coming. I think it's better if you wait until tomorrow."

Justine glanced at Len, who merely returned the look with a sardonic smile. He must have called from his car, once he was sure Justine was on her way.

"Well then." Before she'd died, Justine's mother had drummed politeness into her. She complimented Naomi's kindness as she pushed her chair back from the table. "I'm sorry about the meal. I know you had it prepared with me in mind. Thank you so much, Naomi, but ..."

Len arched one brow. *Running away?* it seemed to say.

Not on your life. She was merely ... regrouping.

After all, in the words of her favorite literary heroine, tomorrow was another day.

CHAPTER SEVEN

Justine was in her room. His mother was in the kitchen, seeing to the proper distribution of the leftovers from that debacle of a meal.

Len had his stepfather all to himself.

At least Walter was sitting up now, unlike earlier, when Justine had arrived. Recently fluffed pillows supported his back. Thin white tufts of hair shot up from his scalp as if he'd been running his fingers through the strands. Flesh pouched beneath his eyes in dark circles. His color was up a bit, rather than the pale imitation of himself he'd presented to Justine.

"Why are you refusing to see her, Walter?"

"I'm not refusing. I just don't like her seeing me like this." Walter fluttered a hand, indicating his face, then the bed.

"Why did you have me bring her all the way down here," he enunciated painstakingly, controlling his irritation, "only to give her less than five minutes with you?"

"You're badgering me, dammit."

In a minute, he'd be doing more than badgering. "She's leaving tomorrow."

Walter's fists clenched in the bedclothes. "You can't let her."

"I got her here. It's up to you to make her stay. And you can't do that if you won't even see her for longer than three minutes."

"It had to have been at least seven."

"Walter."

"All right, all right. I'm thinking."

Len remained patient. With difficulty. The heart attack had affected Walter more than anyone had imagined. The Walter Jarreau he knew had never been so damn wishy-washy. Decisiveness had been his stepfather's stock-in-trade.

"Why don't we make her CFO when Harrison retires in September?" he suggested. "That's her major career goal anyway."

Walter choked.

For a moment, he almost had a heart attack, too. "Should I call nine-one-one?

"I'm fine," Walter managed, though phlegm rattled through his speech. "I refuse to bribe Justine. I want her to come back on her own."

A bit late to hope for that since they'd already thrown her the heart attack whammy.

"Guess that means telling her you plan to put her back in the will isn't an option either?"

"Justine never cared about the money."

Justine Jarreau had only cared about the creep she'd run off with at the age of twenty. Obviously after her money, the little bastard had dumped her as soon as Walter made sure he knew she'd been disinherited. But even after being shown what type of scum she'd chosen over the dreams her father had for her, Justine had refused to come home. Ever.

At least until she thought Walter was lying on his death bed.

For Len, that didn't count as family loyalty.

He'd heard the whole story late one night over a couple of brandies. To put it mildly, he hadn't admired the picture of Justine her father painted. Despite all Walter's excuses for her.

"You're tying my hands, Walter. We have nothing else to offer her."

Walter's head sank back against the pillows. He closed his eyes. All the fight left him as color once again fled his face.

"I'm sure you'll think of something, Len."

He *had* thought of something. He just hadn't wanted to use it. But Walter gave him no choice.

"I'll take care of it."

"I knew you would."

He always had, since the day he'd walked into Jarreau's a little over five years ago.

"You rest, Walter. See her tomorrow. Let her read to you or something sweet like that."

Walter was already asleep as he left and made his way down the corridor to Justine's room.

When she didn't respond to his knock, he found the door unlocked. The bed was empty and undisturbed, but the sound of running water led him to the open bathroom door.

Perfect. She was in the shower. He stepped out of his shoes, yanked his shirt over his head, then tossed it on the floor.

Walter wouldn't let him bribe her with money or a job.

The only leverage he had left was sex.

He'd simply have to seduce Justine into staying.

~

The spray cascaded down her back and over her shoulders. Justine tilted her head back and let the warm deluge wash the shampoo from her hair. Streams of water poured over her breasts. Her nipples tingled.

She didn't need a good imagination to fantasize that it was Len's fingers tweaking, his mouth tugging. All she had to do was remember last night in his hotel room shower. Wet heat rushed between her legs.

She wasn't tired anymore. She wasn't scared about her father's health. She was, considering the circumstances, simply sexually depraved. She shouldn't be having such thoughts at all.

She heard the shower door slide open. She wasn't surprised, nor was she angry. She simply wanted ... him.

He was already naked—and hard. She knew then that he'd stood there and watched her first.

He stepped in and reached for her. She opened her mouth to him and sucked his tongue. She wanted to climb his body, wrap her legs around his waist, and drive down on him. She was merely seconds away from coming.

"Fuck me, Len."

Pulling back, he smiled, then chuckled. "Thought you hated my guts."

"I do. Doesn't mean I don't want you to fuck my brains out."

He pulled her arms from around his neck and stepped back. "Don't rush me."

She reached down, took his cock in her hand and squeezed. Her eyes never left his. His harsh intake of breath was unmistakable. His nostrils flared. He wanted to come as badly as she did.

He pried her fingers off. "Oh, no, you don't. Not now. When I'm really ready. When I'm fucking going to explode."

She pouted. "Then why are you teasing me?"

He grabbed the soap from the dish. "I'm not teasing, babe. I just said I don't want to come yet. You're always rushing me." He soaped up his hands. "Doesn't mean you're not going to come, though."

God, she could orgasm just from the sound of his voice, like syrup drizzled over her, like honey being licked from her breasts.

He backed her up against the tile and lathered her breasts, then her abdomen, and finally the juncture of her thighs. One slick finger breached her folds. He unerringly found her clitoris. Her head fell back against the wall, and she closed her eyes. Two strokes, three. She dug her nails into his shoulders.

"Make me come, Len."

"Oh, baby, I will. Over and over."

He moved aside to let the water beat on her. Then she felt his skin brush the length of her body as he went down on his knees. Then he went down on *her*.

She tangled her fingers in his wet hair and held his face to her mound. Oh God, oh God. His tongue was magic. She lifted one leg to drape it over his shoulder. His body kept her pinned to the wall. The warmth of the water, the heat of his tongue, the kneading of his hands on her thighs—

"Don't stop. Oh God, please don't stop."

And thank God he didn't stop to say he wouldn't stop. She almost giggled hysterically, but at that moment he stuck two fingers straight up inside her, and she went off like the proverbial rocket.

With the last fragment of coherence she had left, she managed not to scream. She rocked against his mouth, undulated on his fingers. And when it was over, she slumped to the floor of the shower.

He leaned back against the wall next to her, the water pounding their legs. "Was it good?"

She smacked him on the arm. "You know it was. But you promised me you were going to make me come over and over. That was only one."

"Did I say I was done?"

"No. I was just curious when you were going to fuck my brains out?"

"Are you this pushy at work?"

"Well, I usually don't beg men to screw my brains out at work."

"Good."

He grabbed her hand, pulled her to feet, and punched off the water. Pulling a scented, plush towel off a heated rack, he rubbed her hair with it.

She'd never experienced anything quite so sensuous.

She knew it was stupid to be doing this. She knew it was some sort of transference thing, feeling awful about her father's health, his new family, his new life, and all she really wanted was someone to make her feel better. Just for a little while. And that someone was Len.

Right time. Right place. Wrong man. But what the hell?

She tugged the towel off her head.

CHAPTER EIGHT

Christ, she was gorgeous. Len couldn't think beyond that one fact.

He didn't care if she was greedy. He didn't care if she was disloyal. He didn't care if she was here only to witness her father's death.

The truth was, he didn't give a goddamn about any of it. He wanted her anyway.

He wasn't doing *this* for Walter's sake. *This* was for him. And for Justine.

He took her ruby lips with his. She moaned into his mouth. Letting the towel drop, he drew her closer, until his cock nestled against her belly. He bent his knees and rubbed against her cleft.

"Christ, you're driving me insane," he murmured.

She opened sultry eyes, the blue deepened to violet with lust. She reached between them and fondled his cock.

"I have a remedy."

Her back was to the door. With her hand manipulating his cock, she backed up, leading him into the bedroom.

Talk about being led around by your dick.

Two feet from the bed she dropped to her knees in front of him. The tip of her tongue delved into the slit at the tip of his cock, licking away a drop of pre-come.

He closed his eyes and tipped his head back, drawing in a deep breath. He definitely wanted to come in her mouth, but not yet.

Dropping a hand to his shaft, he pumped a couple of times, his thumb meeting the seam of her lips. Then he slowly withdrew from the heat of her mouth.

"Got any more of those condoms left?"

Her face reddened, but she nodded, stepped to the bedside table where she'd left her purse. Fishing around, she came up with a foil packet. She tossed it to him.

He ripped it open with his teeth, then smoothed it on, watching her watch him. He pumped his fist a couple of times and his cock grew even larger. Her pupils dilated.

"Come here."

She approached obediently, still mesmerized by his slow fisting of his cock.

"Turn around and get down on all fours."

She did, and he went to his knees behind her and stroked between her ass cheeks with the head of his cock. Then he reached between her legs and dragged his index finger along her slit. She was hot and deliciously wet.

"You want it like this?"

She looked at him over her shoulder, her eyes bright and her lower lip caught between her teeth, and nodded.

Christ, there was something about the power of a woman sticking her ass out for you. The ultimate in trust. He could have done anything, penetrated her in either orifice with any amount of force he chose, and there wasn't much she could have done about it.

Yet, she simply accepted that he wouldn't hurt her.

Sex confirmed so much, even without a word between them. He wondered vaguely why they couldn't communicate like this outside the bedroom.

He eased the tip of his cock inside her pussy lips. She attempted to grind her hips back against him, but his hands controlled her movements. He wanted to enter her slowly, savor every inch, relish the sight.

The position afforded maximum viewing pleasure.

A sigh escaped him as another inch slid inside. Her muscles twitched around him, accommodating, squeezing, inviting him home. She arched her spine and threw her head back. Her nostrils flared with her passion.

"Len, please."

"Patience, baby. You're going thank me when it's all over."

And he'd be thanking God for sending her to him.

He took back the inch he'd given her, then managed three short, sharp thrusts that tantalized the sensitive head of his cock and caused the walls of her vagina to contract around him. Her moisture enhanced the penetration.

"Oh God, Len, please just do it."

He laughed softly. She whimpered and squirmed in his grip, trying to take him deeper. The slow pace of his love-making heightened his every sense, but it was driving her absolutely crazy.

And he craved her madness.

She groaned when he granted her only a scant new inch. But then he leaned forward, wrapping his arm around her, to pinch her nipple. She sucked in a breath. He slid his hand down her abdomen, then delved once more between her lips, finding the little pearl hidden there. She shuddered as he stroked.

"Oh God, Len, please fuck me. Please fuck me." Her words came out like a chant.

He nuzzled her nape. "Not until you beg."

"In case you haven't figured it out." She stopped on a gasp as his finger found a particularly sensitive spot. "That *was* begging."

"Maybe you need to tell me how much it's worth to you?" He insinuated a finger in her, alongside his cock, and caressed her inner tissues. She pulsated around him.

She moaned and shuddered and whimpered. "Your mother was right. You're an ass."

He drew the finger back out, gliding once more across her clit.

She gave an incoherent cry, then grabbed the edge of the bed in front of her and rammed back against him. Her body enveloped his cock straight down to his balls. Her scent rushed to his head, the silkiness of her passage milked him.

And then he was the one who went absolutely and totally fucking insane.

He couldn't get deep enough, couldn't pound hard enough. He wanted inside her, totally inside—inside her heart, her mind, her soul. He wanted to own every inch, touch every centimeter, become a part of her.

His breath rasped in his throat. He covered her mouth with one hand, stifling the primal groans she emitted, and held her hips firmly with the other. Her knuckles turned white where they gripped the bedclothes. And she met him thrust for thrust, jamming back against him, taking him deeper with each plunge.

When she came, she bit the flesh of his palm.

When he came, her name burst from his lips. Then they both collapsed at the side of the bed.

Moments later, or maybe it was hours, she asked, "You don't think anyone heard that, do you?"

"Nah. These walls are too damn thick."

But he didn't give a damn if they had. Before the weekend was out, the whole family would know she was destined to occupy his bed for the foreseeable future.

~

"What on earth was that noise?"

Walter chuckled. "If I don't miss my guess, that was our stallion mounting his mare."

Naomi smacked his arm. "Don't be crude."

"Wasn't the plan to get them to marry?"

"Yes. But that doesn't mean I have to think about our children having sex."

"My love, you are such a prude. And I mean that in the most endearing of ways. Now where the hell is my Yorkshire Pud?"

"Yorkshire Pudding is all starch, and it's cooked in lard. You're lucky I'm letting you eat the roast beef."

"But you cut off the crispy fat around the edges, that's the best part."

"Eat your broccoli."

"I hate broccoli."

"You're lucky I didn't have Mrs. Danaher fix brussels sprouts for Justine."

"I should never have told you they were her favorite. You've been threatening me ever since." But he ate one floweret. "What about a glass of nice burgundy?"

Perched on a chair at the side of the bed, Naomi smoothed her skirt over her knees and ignored the request. "Walter, I don't like this."

"What? Letting me eat red meat?" he said in an attempt to distract her.

"No. Roman said you could have it in moderate portions."

"Miniscule is more like it," Walter muttered.

"It isn't your diet bothering me, and you know it. It's the lying. You didn't see Justine out in the hallway. All the color drained from her face. I think she would have fallen right to the carpet if Len caught her. And Len's really worried, I can tell. This isn't fair to them."

His heart went out to his wife. He hated seeing her upset. So he had to be the strong one. "We're not lying about the heart attack, Naomi. I did have one. Roman says I have to slow down or the next one might kill me or turn me into an invalid."

"Yes, but she thinks you're dying right now."

"We never told her that," he explained as if Naomi were a child. "In fact, I told her twice I was just fine. And you told her, too."

"Walter, you know damn well that while we *say* one thing, you get all sallow and fainty-looking and talk like you're taking your last breath. And while I'm *saying* Roman isn't worried, I'm giving Justine and Len that oh-but-I'm-scared-to-death look." She gulped and her eyes misted. "I hate what we're doing to them. I just hate it."

Jesus H. Christ, the sight of those teary eyes was enough to make him rethink things. *Almost.* Naomi was a woman, with a woman's messy emotions. It was up to him, the man, to put things into perspective for them both.

"So they'll be all the more pleased when they figure out I really am going to recover." He covered Naomi's hand. "It's only for a little while. Just until they fall in love."

"What if they don't? We can't force them, you know."

He looked to the door and smirked. "What we just heard is a damn good start."

She pursed her lips. "That's just sex, Walter."

He smiled lasciviously. "Worked for us, didn't it?"

Her face reddened. "You are a terrible man to remind me about the improper things we did."

He was dying to do them again, every single one of them. The heart attack had made him realize just how much he stood to lose. How everything he loved could be ripped from his grasp at any moment. And how easily that could happen. It had shocked him into realizing he couldn't wait for Justine to come to him, he had to bring her home.

"What's so improper about doing it on the desk in my office?" he teased Naomi, loving the way her face flushed and her breathing increased.

"Because I'm over sixty and you'll be seventy-five next month."

"And a man half my age couldn't have performed better."

She smiled. "You're right. It's the only reason I married you, you little stud muffin."

He pushed the tray aside and patted his lap. "I feel something coming up, my dear. Maybe you should take care of it."

"You are disgusting." But she laughed as she said it, only to sober a moment later. "Len's suspicious. I don't think we're going to be able to fool him for long."

"Then we'll just have to make sure he doesn't spend too much time in here. You'll have to think of ways to keep him busy. With Justine." He patted her hand, surreptitiously pulling her closer at the same time. "We agreed they'd be perfect for each other. We just have to help them figure it out."

"I still don't like the lying. I don't like making them worry more than necessary."

"Neither do I, my pet, but I'm willing to make the sacrifice to ensure their happiness."

"You just wanted a way to bring her home without having to beg."

"I've never denied that. And this little heart attack of mine was the perfect opportunity."

She eyed him gravely. "I'll give it a week. And then I'm telling them the truth."

"Fine, fine," he said with a smile, knowing he could wheedle her around to his way of thinking.

As much as he adored and loved her, she was like all women. Ultimately, they needed to be cosseted and taken care of, told what to think, have all their decisions made for them. Being loved and guided by a man was their whole happiness.

They just didn't like admitting it.

But he did know one thing his gorgeous little nymphet admitted readily to liking very much. "Now, about this little problem I have beneath the covers ..."

CHAPTER NINE

Justine felt ridiculously cheerful as she trotted down the stairs the next morning. She'd been asleep when Len had left her bed, but she'd woken to his scent on the sheets, a stiffness in her muscles, and a faint, yet pleasant, soreness between her legs.

God, what good sex did for a woman's attitude. The man certainly knew how to use the impressive tools the good Lord had given him.

Of course, it was still just sex, she told herself, as she bounded across the hall. Intoxicating, bone-melting, knock-your-socks-off, yes, but *just* sex. Besides, she didn't even like him. He was autocratic, insensitive, and ruthless. Yet, during sex, he did display another side. She had to admit, he was also unselfish, attentive, and appreciative.

How could a man be all those things at once? The characteristics were in total opposition. Weren't they? How could one reconcile his cruelty after that first night and his veneration of his mother?

Plus, how could she account for the things she'd let him do to her? Doggie style, for God's sake! She should have been ashamed, or, at the very least, embarrassed. She wasn't a please-fuck-my-brains-out kind of woman. Until the last two days, the word fuck rarely passed her lips. But she'd wanted the act with every pulsing corpuscle in her body. She'd wanted it with Len, no one else.

Must have been temporary dementia brought on by Len's pitiless disclosure regarding her father's marriage and heart attack, followed by the unsatisfactory reunion itself.

Certainly, that was it.

She didn't quite know how she could face Len this morning. So, she was glad to see the dining room was empty except for Naomi.

The woman's knife and fork were suspended just above her plate as if a thought had suddenly taken control of her in mid-cut. Then she set them down with the chink of metal on china and stared at her still-full dish.

Watching her, Justine's stomach and good mood plunged to her toes.

"Good morning, Naomi."

Her stepmother's attention snapped to her, and the smile suddenly curving her lips appeared painted on. "I do hope you slept well."

Heat swamped her cheeks. While her father lay in his sick bed and Naomi had lain awake, worrying about her husband, Justine had been having the most delectable sexual congress with the poor lady's son.

It was awful. *Justine* was awful.

Naomi didn't seem to notice her lack of answer, instead she pointed to the sideboard. "Help yourself. There's eggs, bacon, potatoes."

"I think I'll just have coffee."

"Oh, Justine, you didn't eat much last night."

No, she hadn't. And now her belly twisted with guilt. For Naomi's sake, she slipped two pieces of toast on a plate.

"How's my father this morning?" she asked.

Naomi looked once more to her half-eaten meal and heaved a sigh.

Justine's pulse rose.

"Did you both sleep well?" *Is my father dying?*

Naomi glanced up, the pasted-on smile once more touching her mouth. "Fine, just fine." Her gaze rose to the point where the ceiling met the molding above the door. "But he's still very tired, you know."

"I'd really like to see him. I'll keep it quiet and restful, though."

Naomi fidgeted with her napkin, twisting it around her fingers, and concentrated on the steam rising from the water pans beneath the serving dishes on the sideboard. "I'm really not sure that's a good idea right now. Perhaps he'll be more rested after lunch." She wet her lips before going on. "I do wish the others would come down. The food's going cold."

And the subject was effectively changed. Even amidst her own chaotic emotions, Justine's heart went out to the older woman. Her stepmother was worried sick over her father's health.

Damn! The audit started tomorrow. Mr. Freidman had practically demanded that she be there.

But there was no way she would leave without spending more time with her father. Nor would she abandon her new stepmother at a time like this. Naomi was on the edge. Justine could tell by the way the woman kept staring at the upper corners of the room, her seemingly scattered thought patterns (who *cared* if the food went cold?), and the abrupt subject changes. Naomi obviously wanted to avoid talking about her husband's condition.

Which scared the crap out of Justine more than teary eyes would have done.

She set her napkin beside her plate. "I'm going to make a phone call, if that's all right."

"Of course, dear. You can use the one in your father's office so you can have a little privacy."

"Thank you. I'll check after lunch to see if my father's well enough for a little visit."

There was really no *if* about it. She would see her father. And she would determine for herself if Naomi was overreacting. Or, if her father's situation was dire.

The image lingering from yesterday's visit did nothing to ease her fears.

~

Justine had simmered throughout lunch. Len had the sense it was more than another postponed tete-a-tete with her father. He'd have to discover what else bothered her later. Right now, he had his mother to deal with.

Suspicion had seeped into his mind.

"Why doesn't he want to see her?" he said as soon as the sight of Justine's perfectly shaped derriere disappeared beyond the doorway.

"It isn't that he doesn't *want* to see her. Of course he wants to. It's that we both feel he needs his rest right now."

"Mother, why aren't you meeting my eyes, here?"

His mother pleated her napkin accordion-style for the third time, and then she met his gaze. "Leonard, I don't like all your questions. I am the mother here, you are the son. Now eat your lunch before it gets cold."

Trust her to try turning the tables on him. "I'm a man, and I know when I'm being manipulated. Now, I want the truth."

This time she picked up her spoon and used the tip to draw patterns on the tablecloth. "He doesn't like her seeing him like this. He just wants to feel a bit stronger."

"I'm not sure how much longer I can get her to stay." It was an empty threat. He'd get her to stay as long as it took, but his mother didn't need to know that.

She bit her lip. "Please, Len, just tell her to be patient a little longer. I'm working on him, I swear it, but he's … well, you know Walter." She rolled her eyes.

Oh yeah, he knew Walter. And Walter was determined to get what he wanted at any price.

"Entertain her, Len, just for a little while. In fact, why don't you take her out to dinner tonight? You can drive her over to the coast. There's that nice little restaurant in Cambria."

He tilted his head to stare at his mother. Her face was flushed. And again, she spoke to her plate instead of to him as she made the bizarre suggestion.

Could the price Walter was willing to pay be his daughter's seduction? Christ, the thought had never occurred to him. Could that be part of Walter's plan? Get his stepson to beguile his daughter long enough to give Walter time to repair the damage done to their relationship fifteen years ago?

Most men couldn't stand to think their daughters might have a sex life. But then Justine was in her mid-thirties, and maybe Walter figured, what the heck, at least it would give him a chance to work on her.

It could be considered sort of sick. Definitely manipulative. But Walter was a master manipulator. Len had witnessed his expertise over and over at the bargaining table.

And after last night, did Len really mind so much? He had come up with the same plan himself. And he wanted her to stay, at least until they'd fully explored this explosive thing between them. He wanted time to figure out why she turned him inside out the moment he put his hands on her.

He wanted her here until the affair had run its course.

Which, given the way his cock had just risen like a flagpole beneath the cover of the tablecloth with the mere thought of another session in his bed, might take a very, very long time.

~

Justine was pissed. And she was terrified.

Freidman, the horse's ass, had actually said, "Tuesday. Or else."

Or else what? He was going to fire her because her father needed her? She could sue his ass for that in today's family-comes-first climate.

But worse than her anger with her boss was her panic as she stood beside Naomi, peering into the older woman's closet. And what a closet. Naomi actually needed a bedroom of her own just to house the enormous quantity of clothing.

And Justine was expected to choose something from the array.

"We'll find the perfect dress for you to wear to dinner," Naomi was saying. "I know you're probably thinking that I'm twenty-five years older than you, and you're going to be stuck wearing some old bag's clothes. But I really do have good taste, my dear, I promise." She scooted a few more hangers along the rod. "You're a little taller than me, but I don't think that matters if we find something calf-length."

"I would never think of you as an old bag, Naomi." And it wasn't her stepmother's taste that worried her or the length of her skirts. It was the gleam in the lady's eyes. The *hope*.

God, the woman thought she was going to stay. How could she tell her she had to leave tomorrow or she wouldn't have a job to go back to?

"Ah, here's one of my favorites." Naomi pulled out a rose-colored dress and held it up against Justine. "Oh, it'll look beautiful." She held it out. "Try it on."

Justine took the dress, dread swimming in the pit of her stomach, as Naomi knelt and rummaged through the bottom of her closet.

"I have the perfect shoes down here somewhere. Ah, there they are." She stood, a pair of four-inch spike heels dangling from her fingers, the leather died to match the dusty rose of the dress exactly.

"Go on, shoo, shoo," she waved her hands, "into the bathroom and try it on."

Justine closed the door, stripped down, and pulled the dress over her head. There was no zipper down the back. One long slit stretched from the top of her spine to the cleft of her buttocks. The only thing that held the dress together at her nape was a carefully hidden hook and eye. The silky fabric draped over her breasts, swirled around her thighs, and caressed her calves. A gold belt linked at her waist. A front split matching the one in back, as if someone had simply forgotten to sew the seams, marched from her throat almost to her belly button. Air-conditioned air sneaked beneath the material both back and front. If she didn't move, though, the gaps were barely visible. But when she did ...

She twisted to the left, then the right, observing what the dress did, then stared at herself in the mirror.

Her panties dampened just thinking about Len's reaction to her in this dress.

"Are you done yet?" Naomi called.

She was afraid to move for fear something might fall out as she walked. "I'm ready."

The door burst open. Naomi gasped. "Oh my. It looks much better on you than it ever did on me."

"I'm not sure it quite covers everything it should."

"Don't be silly. It covers your knees. And bare shoulders are quite acceptable for dinnertime."

"Yes, but …" Justine fingered the material at her throat, held together with a decorative gold clasp that fastened just above the hollow.

Naomi's eyes clouded over. "My goodness, you're beautiful. I always wanted a daughter like you."

A lump clogged Justine's throat. "But you have a daughter."

Naomi smiled through the mistiness of unshed tears. "Of course, I do. And I love her more than anything in the world. But you saw her. Jeans. T-shirt. She doesn't own anything else. She wouldn't wear a dress even to her own wedding."

She swallowed with difficulty. "Naomi, I …"

"Let me think of you as my daughter, Justine. I know we've only just met, and all of this must be so overwhelming for you, but Walter's talked so often about you that I feel like I've known you all your life."

Her stepmother was sweet and well-meaning. But Justine would never be a part of this family. Not really. She'd always be an outsider. That wasn't something she could change after fifteen years on her own.

"Naomi, I have to go back to San Francisco. I have a job."

"I know. But you don't have to go right away. There's plenty of time—"

"I have to leave tomorrow. I've have to be at work on Tuesday. I don't need to leave until late afternoon, though. I can—"

Naomi just looked at her with brimming eyes, and Justine couldn't go on. They stared at each other in the mirror.

"Oh well … of course," Naomi finally murmured. "I just didn't think it would be so soon. Your father …" She stopped.

And Justine knew what would have come next. *Your father's ill. How can you think of leaving?*

Damn Mr. Freidman for being such a demanding dickhead. And damn herself for being such a wimp as to even consider falling for the man's unsympathetic line of crap. He wouldn't fire her. He wouldn't dare.

Would he?

Still, she needed to leave for a host of other reasons. Like Len's effect on her libido. Like her sense of being a third wheel in a house that was overrun with Falconers. Like her confusing emotions, flitting from fear to anger to jealousy in the space of mere seconds.

Friday she'd been totally in control of her emotions and her life.

As of today, her control had been blown to smithereens. She needed it back.

Naomi patted her bare shoulder with a warm hand. "Well, right now, let's not worry about your leaving. Tonight, you're going to be the belle of the ball. Do the shoes fit?"

She stepped into them, and they were perfect. Though she still couldn't quite picture Naomi wearing such a dress nor the matching stiletto heels.

"And here's a darling little evening bag that will do nicely." She slid the gold chain over Justine's shoulder. In the mirror, the beaded bag reflected the glow of the lights and sparkled.

Naomi sparkled just looking at her creation.

The creation just wanted to die.

Instead, she bit her lip and said, "I'll come back next weekend. For sure."

Naomi put both hands to her mouth. "Oh my dear, it would mean so much to your father."

"But he *will* see me tomorrow, even if it's only for a few minutes."

"Of course, of course. I promise. Do you need nylons?"

Justine considered her bare legs and the summer heat outside. "I'll be fine without them."

"Well, I'll just let you toddle off to your room to freshen up and get ready then."

Justine took one last lingering look at her reflection in the mirror.

Len would flip. And then, he'd drag her off to his cave like a Neanderthal. She got wet just contemplating it.

CHAPTER TEN

Jesus H. Christ. "That dress belongs to my *mother*?"

Len and the twins watched, mouths open, as Justine descended.

"Oh my Gawd," Darla finally screeched.

Brian wore a dazed, besotted expression. Len wanted to smack his brother just for looking. And imagining.

On first inspection the dress appeared circumspect enough, though the length flirted with her luscious calves and the neckline bared a sweet expanse of shoulder.

And then she took a step.

A slit emerged from throat to abdomen, the silky material parting infinitesimally to hint at the swell of breasts beneath. A man could slip his hand in that gap and palm the creamy flesh. He could spread the folds of cloth and suck a nipple into his mouth.

Sweet Jesus. He was glad his buttoned dinner jacket hid the sudden rock-like state of his cock.

"You're damn near naked."

His mother appeared at the top of the stairs just beyond Justine. "She is not. You can't see a thing, and you know it."

But the potential was there. His mouth dried up.

"Do not tell me you ever wore that dress in public."

"Leonard, you are such a prude."

"A prude? Just because the thought of my mother parading half-naked—"

He cut himself off because the idea of Justine in the same state of dishabille was having the exact opposite effect. He wanted to throw her down on the carpeted steps, lift her skirt and enter her. Now, without preamble, without foreplay.

And he knew by the sultry, heavy-lidded look on her face, she felt exactly the same way. God help them, they'd never make it to dinner.

He pointed a finger at his mother. "You are never to wear that dress again."

She laughed, then smirked. "To tell you the truth, I haven't worn it in ten years. But it's so pretty, I just couldn't get rid of it."

She smiled down at Justine as the object of his attention turned slightly, revealing more plump breast exposed by the extreme slit. He started to pant.

"You may have the dress, my dear. A little gift."

"But Naomi—"

His mother held up her hand. "Len's right. A sixty-year-old woman shouldn't be wearing something like that."

"That's not what I meant, Mother, and you know it."

"Did you have Roberts bring the car around?"

He'd been just about to issue the instruction. But now ...

"Roberts is in hiding," he lied smoothly. "I'm sure Justine won't mind the short walk to the garage."

He grabbed her hand the moment her feet touched the hall parquet and tugged her into the dining room.

"Len, you don't have to be so forceful," his mother called.

"The reservation's for 7:00. We'll be late if we don't hurry," he answered from the door to the kitchen. They'd be damn lucky if they arrived in time for the 8:00 reservation he'd actually made.

"Well, have a good time."

He would. Justine would. If he didn't lose it before they ever got to the garage.

They passed through the kitchen amidst open mouths and speculative gazes and down the hall to the back entrance. The second he'd slammed the garage door behind them, he pulled her into his arms and stuck his tongue down her throat. His hands found their way into that miraculous dress and kneaded her breasts.

Justine moaned and hooked her leg around his hip. The silly little purse fell to the concrete floor. He continued exploring the scrumptious globe with one hand while the other slipped beneath the flouncy skirt. Her thigh was tantalizingly bare. He skimmed the satiny flesh in search of his ultimate destination. He cupped one butt cheek bared by thong panties, then squeezed and molded her to his palm. And his rigid cock.

She nipped his lower lip and went up on tiptoe to wrap her arms around his neck. And then she drove her tongue into his mouth once more.

It was then he discovered that she'd dressed for the evening sans panties. Not a thong, as he'd thought. Just sweet flesh begging him to enter.

Sweet Holy Jesus, he was going to die. He followed the cleft of her buttocks to the warm cream of her pussy. She drenched his fingers. His cock pulsed and throbbed. He wanted inside her, wanted to mark his territory with his scent and his jism. He rocked against her, bringing them both closer to the edge.

He could come without being inside her. Without even her hands or her mouth on his cock. He'd gotten that hot for her in something like two minutes flat.

A premature ejaculator he'd never been. He wasn't about to start now. Sex was for savoring, not rushing. He pulled back from her lips, removed his hands from her breast and her pussy, and allowed her foot to descend back to the floor.

She stared at him with a bewildered, passion-drugged gaze.

He cupped her face in his hands as he ran his tongue lightly along the seam of her lips.

"Too fast," he murmured. "We need to slow it down, enjoy it."

"I was enjoying it."

He nipped on her lower lip, then sucked the plump flesh into his mouth. He nibbled, licked, blew on the wet skin.

"I was about to come in my pants."

She nuzzled his throat, then bit down on a morsel of flesh. "So?"

"When I come, it'll be when I'm inside you, either your body or your mouth."

"Promises, promises." She breathed against his earlobe, sending a jolt of electricity to his groin. His cock jumped.

With his hands on her delectably bare shoulders, he propelled her back against his car, passenger side. Then he lifted her, planting her butt on the metal just over the wheel well.

"Oh, that's cold."

"It won't be for long." He nudged her legs apart and stepped between them. One shoe clattered to the floor.

"Your mother's shoe, it might get dirty."

"Screw the shoe."

A tiny dimple creased the corner of her mouth. "I thought you wanted to screw *me*."

"I do. And I'm going to." He parted the dress, exposing both breasts with their beaded nipples.

"Right here?"

"Exactly here."

He bent his head and tugged one nipple into his mouth. Her fingers flexed on his shoulders, her nails pressing through the jacket.

"But we can't do it right here. Anyone could walk in on us."

Despite her protests, she arched her back to give him better access. In reward, he lightly pinched her other nipple. With a last flick, he raised his head.

"No one's going to come out here until they see my car leave."

"But you don't think they think ..."

He thrust a hand beneath her dress and hit his target the first time. Her legs twitched, she gulped in a breath, and the sultry perfume of her desire floated up to him.

"I don't care what they think. I can't wait." He stroked the swelled nub of her clit, bathed it with her own juices. "Can you?"

"Your mother's dress will get dirty."

He removed his touch long enough to rip off his coat and throw it on the hood behind her. "My jacket will protect it."

He worked his belt free, then tugged his zipper down. Her legs clasped his hips and pulled him closer.

"You know, I really don't like you." She took his cock in her hand and smoothed a thumb over the crown.

"I don't like you either."

"Good." Then she smiled, her thumb still working the tiny slit on his tip. "I just thought we ought to get that little something straight between us."

He arched one brow. "Little?"

She stroked him. "I meant big."

He took control of his own tool. He swabbed the inner walls of her pussy with a finger, then lubricated himself. Then he reached in his pants pocket for the requisite foil package.

"You brought a condom to a fancy dinner that your mother arranged?"

He grinned. "You never know when something might come up."

"I think you're a slut."

He ripped the packet open, removed the article and sheathed himself. "And I think you like that I'm a slut very much."

"This is just sex, you know."

"I know." He nudged her tunnel with his aching dick.

"I'm leaving tomorrow." She bit her lip as he entered with one restrained thrust.

He put his finger to her clit and his lips to her mouth, and then he moved inside her.

She moaned. "This is the last time, you know, the very last time."

"Why don't you just shut up and kiss me," he muttered before he captured her tongue with his.

Then he fucked the hell out of her, infinitely harder, faster, and better than the night before. If that was possible. She screamed when she came. Only his hand over her mouth contained the sound.

But nothing could contain the impact when he hit his own peak right on the heels of hers.

He wouldn't let her leave tomorrow or the day after. Nor this week or the next. Despite her shallowness, her greed, her disregard for the importance of family.

He might never be able to let her leave at all.

CHAPTER ELEVEN

"Why'd it take them so long to get the car started?" Brian asked as all three stood at the dining room window, watching Len's car disappear around a curve in the driveway.

"Duh," Darla muttered.

Naomi let a tiny smile touch her lips. Worry dashed it only moments later.

Sex wasn't love. Justine would leave. And Walter would never get the chance to realize he needed to apologize for what he'd done to his daughter all those years ago.

~

"This isn't some weird Oedipal thing, is it? Like, you see me in your mother's dress and want to do me."

Seated to her left, his knee brushing hers intimately beneath the table, Len laughed. "I'd kill her before I'd let her out in public wearing that dress. If I'd known she was hiding that in her closet, I'd have stolen it and burned it on the front lawn.

But I certainly wouldn't do it from any weird Oedipal complex."

The low buzz of diners surrounded them. Candles flickered and the scent of a tasteful vase of freshly cut flowers perfumed the air. Waiters hovered at the edges of the exclusive dining room, waiting for the slightest signal from their patrons.

Justine sipped the expensive merlot Len had ordered. "Aren't you even insulted that I'd bring it up?"

"No. You hate my guts, remember? I'd expect nothing less."

But that was the crux of the problem. She hadn't hated his guts last night, despite what she'd tried to tell herself. She hadn't hated him in the garage.

Her face flamed. God, how could she have done that? He hadn't even locked the door. Anyone could have walked out there. She just hadn't cared. That's how badly she'd wanted him inside her.

That sure as hell didn't sound as if she hated the man.

She swirled her beef cutlets in their cream sauce and decided it didn't bear thinking about. She was going home soon. She'd forget about him, except for the occasional visit down to check on her father. Maybe Christmas and Thanksgiving every year. Len would eventually show up with a wife. And then a couple of dark-headed little munchkins. Probably twins. Except that the man was a ruthless executive married to his job. Oh God.

She pushed the plate away. The attentive waiter appeared immediately to relieve her of the messy dishes.

"Could I get that in a to-go box, please?" she said, smiling up at him.

He stared as if she'd suddenly sprouted a second head.

She raised both brows. "A people bag, maybe?"

Three deep lines furrowed his previously smooth forehead.

"A doggie bag?" Finally, she threw up her hands. "Just put it in a plastic bag so I can take it home, okay?"

"As Madame wishes," then he whisked the plate away with such a flourish that she knew the kitchen would be in an uproar at her request.

Len toyed with the stem of his wineglass. "You know, we do have food at the house. You don't need to bring home your leftovers."

"When you have only yourself to depend on, you learn not to waste anything." From necessity, she'd adopted the doggie-bag habit her first year out of college, when brown-bagging lunch while on an audit simply wasn't done; the inclination had not expired with the comfort of her controller's salary.

"Even when someone else is paying for the meal?"

"Especially when someone else is paying."

He gazed at her intently, and she regretted the remark. It said way too much about the fifteen years she'd been on her own.

"Penny for your thoughts," he said just when the silence between them had been about to drive her crazy. Or make her reveal something else she didn't want him to know.

She strove for a subject they wouldn't fight about. "I'm worried about your mother."

"My mother?" he repeated as if he'd hadn't been expecting that one at all.

"She doesn't seem to be dealing with my father's illness. Not at all. I mean, she sent me out on a date like I was Cinderella or something while my father is lying near death just down the hall." She scrunched her nose. "Why do they have separate rooms, by the way?"

Len's eyes flattened to the color of dark, overturned earth. "Are you implying that my mother doesn't care enough for your father?"

"No, I didn't mean that. I just meant that it seems like she's pretending nothing is wrong. When something is obviously very wrong if he sends me that sort of frantic letter, then he can't even see me once I'm here."

"I think it's won't, not can't."

"I don't get it."

Len muttered something beneath his breath.

"What did you say?"

"I said, I don't get it either."

She tipped her head to one side and stared at his strong face. A worry line creased his forehead. Another slashed down between his eyebrows.

"You really don't know what's going on, do you?"

He didn't answer. Whatever he thought or felt, he didn't want to share with her.

Not unusual. Just because you spread your legs for a man didn't make you his confidant. It just made you his latest conquest. She almost choked on the bitterness. She really wasn't a bitter woman. She couldn't have said where this strange feeling came from. *All* the strange feelings she'd experienced since the night he'd come for her. Jealousy, anger, resentment. They'd never been part of her repertoire.

Until her father got sick.

Until she'd met Len.

"Maybe you ought to tell me everything about his heart attack."

He looked up, pierced her with a pointed glare. "He had it a week ago. At the office. In the middle of a board meeting. It wasn't faked, if that's what you're getting at."

"I'm not." Was she? "I'm just wondering if something else is going on. I really want to talk with his doctor."

"I've talked to his doctor. It's exactly as my mother says. Walter needs rest and a lightening of his load. That's all."

"Then why, the night we first met, did you lead me to believe he was dying?"

The question lay on the table between them like an uninvited guest.

Finally, he said, "Is that what I did?"

"Yes."

"As I recall, I merely told you he couldn't continue at his current pace."

"There was what you said. And the *way* you said it." There was the way he'd showed up at her door in the morning, his insistence. And of course, her father's letter, the one Len had seen fit to hand-deliver as if time were of the essence. Except that a phone call could have done the job.

He leaned back in his chair, gripped his glass by the stem and tipped the last of his wine down his throat. It was not the action of a connoisseur nor that of a winemaker.

It was the act of a man avoiding answers.

~

She had him by the balls. He couldn't define Walter's condition. He wasn't completely sure of it himself anymore. And he certainly couldn't tell her how he'd planned and executed her seduction. Not if he wanted her back in his bed this very night.

Nor did he wish to lie to her anymore.

He strove for compromise.

"It was important to me that you come home."

"Why?"

"Because I care about Walter. I want to help him get what he needs."

She stared at him a long time, looking as if she thought somehow she might be able to see inside his head and judge his intentions.

"You love my father, don't you?"

Love? He'd never thought of it in those terms. He revered Walter. He was grateful for his mother's happiness. He was appreciative of the faith Walter bestowed upon him as he stood at the helm of the Jarreau family business.

"He's part of my family now."

Her lips curved in a smile that didn't make it as far as her eyes. "Ah yes, family. It's very important to you."

"It's *all*-important to me."

"Were your parents divorced?"

"My father died."

"How old were you?"

"I was twenty-two. The twins were ten."

"That's a young age for you to take on such an awesome responsibility."

It amazed him that she understood him well enough to know he *had* taken it on.

"Had you graduated college?"

"Just."

"And you went to work for my father when?"

He answered her rapid fire questions succinctly, revealing no emotion. It seemed the safest approach. "Five years ago."

"When did they start dating?"

"Four years ago."

"It took them a long time to get married."

"I wouldn't know about that decision."

"Do you miss your father?"

"Do you miss yours?" He ended the interrogation.

She pursed her lips. "Touché. Successful parry, Mr. Falconer."

"What about my questions?"

"I thought you already knew all the answers."

"I do." He knew her mother, adored by Walter as well as his daughter, had died when Justine was ten. That fact reminded him of the twins. Except that *they* hadn't lost a loving parent. They'd actually been the lucky ones, though they hadn't realized that at the time, perhaps did not even understand that now. But *he* knew. "I just haven't heard your version yet."

"I left. You and your family came. End of story."

He searched for a trace of bitterness or envy, either in her eyes, on her face or in her voice. He found none. But then, she was an executive. And she was her father's daughter. A better poker-faced player than that man, Len had never seen. Except for himself.

So far, he had yet to fully grasp Justine's feelings about anything. Other than sex.

Sexually, he was master between them, the one in control. He knew that. He could probably get her to acknowledge the fact with a nod of her head. He could have her anywhere he wanted, any way he wanted, any time. For Christ's sake, chances were, she'd let him put his hand up her dress right now beneath the table cloth and bring her to orgasm in the middle of the dining room.

But he'd lose her the moment she patted her clothes back into place.

Which meant he'd never really had her at all. Not in any meaningful sense.

And he was goddamn sick of it.

"Let's go." He threw a few bills on the table, more than enough to cover the check and a generous tip, then pulled her to her feet without actually offering her his hand. The slit in her dress gaped. She held it together with a palm to her chest.

"But my leftovers—"

"Forget the damn doggie bag."

As he damn near dragged her from the dining room, he felt the proprietary surge of a male lion, but managed to stop short of a full-throated roar.

CHAPTER TWELVE

As they crossed the brightly lit parking lot, Len handed her the keys to the Jag. "You drive."

"I'm not driving your car."

"I've had too much wine. You wouldn't want me to get arrested on a DUI, would you?"

He hadn't had more than two glasses. If that. Justine frowned, trying to remember for sure. Had they even finished the extravagantly priced bottle he'd ordered?

She took the keys only because she didn't want to fight about it. The man definitely had his mind made up. What had started out as a pleasant evening—all right, it had started out explosively, then mellowed to pleasant—had now become somewhat dangerous.

She had so many questions, and Len hadn't given her a single answer. Sure he'd given her dates and facts. He was the archetype for the "just the facts, Ma'am" stereotype. But how had he felt about his father's death? Why were his siblings so much younger? Why had he never married?

The first question she'd asked which required an answer bordering on the emotional, he'd turned the tables on her.

Then again, why on earth did she want to examine his emotions anyway?

She beeped the remote, and Len opened the door for her. His eyes simply ate her up as she slid into the seat. There was no other way to describe his hot gaze as her dress parted once more to reveal the slope of her breasts and a bit of bare midriff. She hadn't worn a bra; the dress didn't allow it.

Suddenly the idea that she did the driving didn't seem so bad. At least then she wouldn't embarrass herself by making some bizarre pass at him in the car. She'd been right Saturday morning when she'd insisted on taking her own car. Sequestered in the close confines of his luxury vehicle, her blood fairly hummed through her veins and her legs trembled with desire. She would have been a goner after four hours. The darkness tonight only intensified the feeling.

"Remember the way back?"

"Mmm," was her only answer as she fidgeted with the buttons, searching for the right seating arrangement.

"Good." Then he leaned back against the headrest and closed his eyes.

She pulled out of the parking lot and hit the road. He'd laced his fingers in his lap and settled in. The sweet silence in the car, punctuated only by the soft sound of his breathing, soothed her nerves.

She shouldn't have started with the questions. That's when everything started to go wrong. Perhaps he'd thought she was attacking his mother. Or being nosy. Which certainly put their relationship in prospective. She was a decent fuck, but God forbid he should share anything else with her.

But he did share something else with her. History. It hadn't escaped her notice that his father had died at approximately the same time her father had "disinherited" her for not falling in with his plans. She and Len had experienced a great deal of upheaval at just about the same stage of life.

It had turned him into an egocentric despot who thought he knew what was best for everyone around him.

It had turned her into a lonely career woman who sought solace in the arms of a one-night-stand.

She could admit now that what she'd really been searching for was far more than a night of passion. She was tired of the loneliness. She just wasn't sure she could assuage it with Len. Or that she'd even want to try.

She turned her head slightly to evaluate his sleeping face.

But he was awake. His deep coffee-colored eyes glittered in the flash of oncoming headlights. Watching her, he'd half-turned in his seat. His right hand massaged his impressive hard-on.

Her heart stuttered, skipped a beat. Between her legs, moisture blossomed. She had the irresistible need to cross her legs, pressing them together to enhance the sensation. Thank God she was the one doing the driving, and thus the one in control.

"You have an extraordinary profile."

The size of that erection suggested he'd been examining more than her profile.

"Your nipples are hard."

They burgeoned against the soft material. His eyes on them initiated a tingle that vibrated through her belly. She swallowed, but her throat remained painfully dry. With a glance in the rearview mirror, she saw that her pupils had dilated.

And then he reached across with his right hand, abandoning his cock, to rub the pad of his index finger around her nipple.

She shivered and bit her lip. "Don't do that while I'm driving."

"Why? Does it make you feel like you're going to lose control?"

"No, it just—"

He cupped her breast and squeezed, manipulating the nipple between his thumb and forefinger. "It's just what?"

It made her thirsty. It made her hot. It made her want to yank the wheel to the right, stomp on the brake and ram the transmission into Park so that she could throw herself across the console at him.

"It's a little distracting is all."

In the dark, she could almost feel his satisfied smile as if it were a touch.

His hand slipped inside the slit of her dress and wandered over the flesh of her abdomen. Her belly contracted.

"Have you ever given a man a blow job while he's driving?"

Another spurt of moisture creamed her inner walls. "No."

He laughed softly "Now *that's* distracting."

She wanted to ask what it felt like. She couldn't imagine having an orgasm while trying to concentrate on the road.

He removed his hand from inside her dress and placed it on her knee. Then he answered her unspoken question. "It's like you're split in two. You want to close your eyes and scream." His hand sneaked beneath the hemline, raising her skirt to caress her thigh." And yet you've got to keep them wide open." He slipped closer to her apex, molding the flesh of her inner thigh to his palm. "Everything's ... brighter, sharper." He stroked her curls. She held her breath. "And then you can't seem to stop coming. And you hold onto the wheel so tightly you think it's going to crack in your grip."

Her dew soaked the dress. She clutched the wheel as tightly as he depicted.

"Want me to show you what it's like?"

"No." The single word rasped from her throat.

"Spread your legs," he whispered.

God, she was so hot. She wanted his fingers inside her. She wanted to break apart just the way he described.

And then he parted her thighs. His finger found her creamy surface, delved deep inside. She shuddered as he withdrew. Her hands involuntarily jerked on the steering wheel. Her legs tensed, pushing down against the carpet and the accelerator. The car jumped forward.

"See what I mean?" he whispered. "You can't control it. Yet you *have* to control it."

She backed off the gas as he slid a finger across her clit. A low moan escaped her throat. "Oh my God."

"Not God. Me. I'm the only one right here next to you. Does my touch make you absolutely fucking crazy?"

His touch centered now on her clitoris, smearing her wetness around and around. Rhythmically. Achingly. Her bottom came off the seat, her hips rotated in the opposite direction of his touch, and her head fell back until she was staring at the road through nothing more than the slits of her eyelids.

He slid back inside, skimming a sensitive spot that made her legs cramp and her bottom leap.

Air rushed out of her lungs, and she started to pant. She was all over the fricking road. Her sweaty palms slid across the wheel. The dance of her hips was uncontrollable.

"Please stop, oh God, please stop."

"You don't want me to stop. You want me to make you come all over the seat. You want me to finger-fuck you until you're screaming and you don't give a damn if you kill us in the process. You want to come, don't you? Go ahead, come. Fuck my hand. Suck my fingers in. Do it. Do it. Now. You know you want to. You can't help it."

And then she couldn't stop the rush. She screamed, and the car careened across the median, then back to the shoulder. Gravel spewed from beneath the tires, and still she came, screaming his name and obscenities she hadn't even known were harbored in her subconscious.

The car came to a rest at the side of the road, half on the shoulder, half in a ditch. She didn't remember putting her foot on the brake.

Her breath rushed from her lungs, her body trembled, and a sheen of perspiration cooled against her flaming skin.

"Oh my God, how could you do that to me?"

His hand remained between her legs, petting, soothing. "It was easy."

"Bastard."

She was shaking. He pressed a kiss to her ear, tasted her lobe.

"But you liked it. And you'd let me do it again, wouldn't you? I wonder what else you'd do for me? Only for me."

"You're crazy."

He grabbed her chin and turned her to face him. "Maybe. But your answer intrigues me."

"I don't care for the question."

He sealed her lips with his, sucking her tongue into his mouth.

With her hand around his wrist pushing him off, she said, "You drive. I don't feel like it anymore."

"You mean you *can't* drive after the way you just exploded against my fingers. You can't even stand up. Because it was so damn good."

She yanked on the door handle and climbed out. With one hand on the roof of the car, she leaned down to peer at him. "I can stand up just fine. But with you driving, your hands will be occupied."

He smiled and his teeth gave off a feral gleam. "Are you sure you don't want them otherwise occupied?"

She couldn't say why she was so damn angry. It had been the best, the absolute best, orgasm she'd ever had. Freaking *ever*. And yet … she sensed something calculating in his touch, something made quite clear in his declarations afterward.

He'd been manipulating her, and more than in just the physical sense. He'd been attempting to work over her emotions as well as her body.

And she'd be damned if she'd let him touch her again.

"Either you drive or I walk."

He raised his hands in mock surrender. "Fine. But if *you* want to give me a blow job while I'm driving, that's fine with me."

"In your dreams."

Good exit line. The trouble was, whether she did it or not, the blow job *would* be in her dreams. And there wasn't a damn thing she could do to stop that.

~

It hadn't worked, goddamn it. He proved only what he already knew. That he could have her body. He wasn't sure she'd give him anything else.

But what else was it he wanted?

Easy. He wanted her to stay. For Walter's sake, of course. But also to see this thing between them through.

He'd considered asking her if she'd stay through the entire week. He hadn't because he knew she'd only verify she was leaving on Monday, as she'd told his mother.

The episode in the car hadn't made a damn bit of difference to that. All it had done was leave him with an aching SRH. Semen retention headache. Something a cold shower would have no effect on. Sure, he could jack off. After all, a man's hand was his own best friend in the middle of the night.

But he wanted Justine's hand gripping his cock, her mouth sucking him, her body taking his all the way.

But he wouldn't get his wish tonight.

After he'd politely walked her to her bedroom, she'd closed the door softly in his face before he even finished saying goodnight. It would have been better if she'd slammed it. Then he'd heard the lock click. Of course, he could have gotten in. But it was the unspoken message. Stay away. He could have ignored that as well. But he knew his biggest mistake to date would be forcing his way in.

Christ. He really didn't get why she was so angry about the car thing.

Fuck! Of course, he got it. She saw right through his methods to the underlying meaning, which was that he wanted to dominate. He'd wanted to master her inside and out. And she wasn't about to be mastered.

He needed another approach.

The idea came to him halfway down the corridor to his own room. He snapped his fingers.

Yeah. That was the ticket. Walter didn't want to bribe her with a job. But Len had no such compunction. Tomorrow, he'd seduce her with the thing she'd always wanted.

Then he'd show her *everything* she stood to gain if she stayed.

CHAPTER THIRTEEN

Justine wouldn't be put off. She glanced at her watch. "It's nine o'clock, Naomi. I'll only spend fifteen minutes with him, but I will have those fifteen minutes."

Naomi patted her arm in conciliation. "Of course, you will, dear. I didn't mean to make it sound like you wouldn't. Let me just go see if he's finished his breakfast."

Goosebumps peppered arms bared by the thin cotton sundress she'd worn. The physical reaction might have been to the cool, dark-paneled interior hallway. Or it might have been the prospect of seeing her father, more precisely, the fear of seeing his poor condition once more confirmed with her own eyes.

Naomi skittered down the hall and tapped on the door. "Walter, dear, Justine's here to see you. Yes, dear." She turned back and held up one finger, then slipped inside the door and closed it.

Irritation bubbled to the surface. She crossed her arms over her chest and tapped her toe against the hall carpet.

"Good morning, Justine."

She started at the sound of his voice behind her. She'd thought he'd be at work by this time on a Monday morning. Despite a stepfather's illness.

Schooling her features into a neutral façade, she turned. "Good morning, Len."

His gaze traveled her length, from naked shoulders to exposed legs, and lingered. Heat swelled in the depths of his eyes. "I hope you slept well."

He looked exceptionally good in a charcoal suit and tie. Her heart rat-a-tatted. "Yes, thank you. And you?"

"Better than I expected to."

It was a reference to what had happened between them last night. She decided to make it the only one. "I'll be leaving after I've seen my father. Naomi's checking on him now."

Len frowned, then reached to adjust his tie. "I thought you'd want to drop by the winery. To see what changes have occurred since you were there."

She never wanted to see the winery again in her whole life. She was afraid if she did, she'd lust after it as she had in her teens, in the days when she'd imagined someday it would be hers. "Thanks, but no thanks."

"It would make your father happy."

So, he was playing the "happy daddy" card? Well, she hadn't lain sleeplessly in her bed last night for nothing. She'd thought about what Len had done to her. And she'd thought about her father. And the conclusion she'd reached was that Len hadn't done anything bad to her. She'd participated, and she'd had the best damn orgasm in recorded history. So what if it was in a car? And so what if he'd had some other agenda? She'd been in control of receiving "the best damn orgasm."

And as for her father, he had another agenda, too. She could let him lead her around by the short hairs, to use the male vernacular, or she could take charge and force herself into his sickroom. After which, she could get back to her real life, which, thank God, wasn't peopled with anyone more complicated and dangerous than Dickhead Freidman.

As for Len in the here and now, engaging in a power struggle with him over whether she would or would not go to the winery would put him in control once more. That she refused to allow. In fact, the same reasoning could be applied to staying angry over last night's orgasm. If she was angry, then the sex meant something. And it didn't. Ergo, any residual ire had to be squashed.

She mentally dusted off her hands. "Fine. I'd love to see the winery again. Fond memories, you know."

Len narrowed his eyes, obviously searching for the hidden knife in her easy acquiescence. But she'd wrested control and all he could say was, "How about two o'clock?"

Naomi stuck her head out the door and signaled with a hand wave.

Justine turned back to Len. "Make it ten-thirty. I'm leaving for the Bay Area no later than three." And then she left, snubbing him in favor of her father.

The sensation was delicious. Almost as delicious as the orgasms she'd *allowed* him to give her.

~

Len observed his mother and Justine from the hallway.

"I just wanted to clean up his breakfast tray before you came in," his mother said in a hospital-like whisper as she finally allowed her stepdaughter into the inner sanctum.

God, Justine was magnificent. He had suspected it before. He was sure of it now. She'd bested him. He had to admit that. But damn if he hadn't enjoyed it. Almost as much as he'd enjoyed fingering her to orgasm last night in the car. What a woman.

Life with her would never be dull.

Life with her? Christ. He wasn't planning commitment here. Just mutual satisfaction for a mutually agreeable period of time.

The problem was, he realized, that he could see no foreseeable end to that agreeable period of time.

~

Naomi balanced the breakfast tray on her hand. A cloth napkin covered the remains of the meal as if to hide Walter's lack of appetite. Naomi smiled wanly and whisked through the door.

"I'll be back in a moment," she murmured, then closed the door behind her.

Justine pulled a straight-backed chair to the side of the bed, easing into it as she let her gaze wander over her father's features.

His eyes were closed, and his hands were clasped over his chest. The pale skin, revealed in shadows cast by the dim bedside lamp, could have been that of a dead person. But there, she saw a slight flutter of nose hair as he breathed.

"Hi, Dad."

His lids lifted slowly. "Sweetheart," he said with a thin, reedy whisper.

"How are you feeling?"

"Oh, much better."

She took his hand. Her heart wrenched. "Much better" didn't describe the weak grip he gave her fingers. His long rest periods didn't seem to be helping him.

"I don't believe you, Dad. Tell me the truth."

His gaze darted about the room, then fixed on the slit of morning sunlight streaming through the curtains. "I am telling you the truth."

"Then maybe you need to get out of this room. I think you at least need some sunlight."

"No," he said in the strongest voice she'd heard out of him yet, and the clutch of his hand suddenly found its strength. "I mean, the sun hurts my eyes."

The swish of the opening door sounded behind her. Naomi's flowery perfume wafted gently over them.

"Don't you think we ought to open the curtains and the windows, Naomi? I'm sure it would do him a world of good." The lack of fresh air could be a reason behind his pallid flesh.

"I think that's a wonderful idea, Justine." Naomi's eyes twinkled, and she gave her husband a slick smile.

"I'm feeling tired again," he said, his voice quavering. "Perhaps you could come back this afternoon?"

She sighed. "I have to leave this afternoon, Dad."

"Leave?" he croaked.

"We're in the middle of an audit." She stopped. The explanation wouldn't satisfy him, she knew. She wasn't sure it satisfied her. "But I told Naomi I'd be back this weekend."

"Len's taking her by the winery this morning before she leaves," Naomi said, still with that strangely slick smile on her face.

"This weekend?" he murmured.

Justine squeezed his hand. "I promise. I'll leave right after work on Friday so that we can have two whole days together."

"But—"

"You said you needed a nap, Walter." Naomi pried his hand from Justine's. "She'll say goodbye before she leaves, won't you, Justine?"

"Of course."

She rose from the chair and backed to the door while her father's attention was riveted on Naomi.

"It's nappy-nappy time, Walter dear."

He mumbled something Justine couldn't hear.

She had hoped to feel better after seeing him. Instead her stomach felt tied into a morass of tiny knots.

~

"She's leaving," Walter shouted. He quieted immediately, worried that Justine might have heard him.

Naomi sat down in Justine's vacated chair. "She said she'd be back on the weekend, and she will be. Have faith in her."

He had plenty of faith. Faith in his ability to get Justine to see reason if he could just find the right button to push. And weekend visits weren't the ticket. Once she realized the heart attack was no big deal, those visits would dwindle.

But he knew better than to use the words "no big deal" within Naomi's earshot. With her, better to exploit the little time bomb. "I could have died. Doesn't that mean anything to her?"

"Yes, dear, I'm sure it does. But she's got a life, a job. She can't just ignore her responsibilities. You wouldn't want her to. She wouldn't be the woman you raised if she did."

"If I'd died, they would have given her at least a week off."

His wife crooked one eyebrow. "As I recall, Jarreau company policy grants only three days for bereavement."

Naomi had been in human resources. She'd updated the employee manual. "It does?" He feigned ignorance. "We'll have to have Len look into that."

She pursed her lips and gave him that look, the one she affected when her patience with him wore thin. "Darling, just trust her. It will all work out."

"The last time she went away, she never came back," he whined. Whining was a rarely used tactic, one best employed only with females in the immediate family. Where Justine was concerned, he'd use anything in the arsenal.

"And whose fault was that, Walter?"

He regretted telling his wife the complete story of Justine's abandonment. Naomi viewed the whole incident from a woman's perspective. They always spouted those words, freedom and independence, as if they thought they'd been slaves or something.

"All I ever wanted to do was give her the best things life had to offer."

"But *you* decided what those things were to be."

"I tried to guide her. She was so young." And she hadn't appreciated his helpfulness. "What else was I supposed to do? Let her ruin her life?"

"You blackmailed her, Walter."

"That's a very strong word." He'd simply applied a series of monetary incentives to show her where she'd gone wrong. The plan had backfired.

"You told her who to marry, and you tried to take away her ability to be independent."

All right, those were Naomi's hot buttons. She'd married for security, the husband handpicked by her well-to-do parents, the wedding the event of the decade. It hadn't worked well. It had, in fact, been disastrous, though Naomi, sweet woman that she was, had always used phrases like "unfortunately mismatched" and "not meant-to-be."

If Len were to be believed, the man had been mentally and verbally abusive. Luckily, he'd died before it became physical. Though sometimes he wished Ronald Falconer had lived so that he could beat him to a bloody pulp for the abuses he'd heaped on Walter's beloved.

With her son's support, guidance and aid, Naomi had found her way out of the mire.

And Len was just the kind of man Justine needed to guide her.

If Walter could get her to see that.

"I've learned my lesson. If she could just forgive me." He wrung his hands, a gesture designed to garner Naomi's sympathy.

Naomi stood. "Maybe you need to actually admit to yourself that you were wrong before anybody can forgive you."

He didn't like the sound of that. If he didn't know better, he'd think it was an admonishment. He put a hand to his left arm and rubbed. *Absently*, as if he really didn't notice he was doing it.

Maybe it was better not to tell his beloved wife the next step in his campaign to get Justine home for good.

CHAPTER FOURTEEN

Len finished the tour with a visit to the boardroom. The space had been renovated since her time, furnished with a huge mahogany conference table, leather chairs and a wet bar.

"Would you like a drink?" Len indicated the mini-fridge with a flourish.

"You dispense alcohol during working hours?"

"I was offering a soda or juice." He glanced down at her legs. "Though I can think of a few other things I'd like to offer as well."

Justine stepped behind the barrier of the chairman's seat at the head of the table. "Apple juice will be fine."

He popped the top on a can, poured it into a cut-glass tumbler and handed it to her. His fingers brushed hers during the transfer, deliberately, she was sure, if that predatory gleam in his eyes meant anything.

"So, what do you think of the place?"

What she thought was that they ought to just change the family name from Jarreau to Falconer right now and be done with it. He'd been treated with deference, even awe. Though he'd allowed his brother, Brian, to conduct the actual tour, including the aging caves and tasting room, all eyes had been on Len throughout. Brian had seemed ecstatic to be given the "honor." He'd been knowledgeable, responsible and bright with the enthusiasm of youth.

She didn't know any of the employees. And they had to be told she was Walter Jarreau's daughter.

There'd been a time when she'd been on a first-name basis with every single person that worked for her father. Her "family" had been vast. She'd planned spending a lifetime with them inside the fragrant facility and in the vineyards.

But Len had changed everything about the place. Better manufacturing flow, just-in-time purchasing and planning, he'd claimed. As if they made widgets instead of wine. She'd remained dumbfounded amidst the lively discussion at the bottling line of cork versus screw caps and the cost of retooling. Screw caps? Next, they'd be considering box packaging. No wonder her father'd had a heart attack.

Thank God, Len hadn't insisted on taking her to the vineyards. She'd probably have had her own heart attack at the changes he'd made out there.

Then there'd been Darla and the new label. The girl's excitement had been palpable, like the hum of an electric current.

Justine had hated the flash of resentment and jealousy she felt. But she couldn't deny it. She wasn't part of Jarreau's anymore, hadn't been for fifteen years.

Not that it mattered. She was leaving today. She'd be back next weekend as she'd promised her father and maybe a few weekends after that, depending on how he fared. But she'd never set foot in the winery again.

It hurt too much.

"Very interesting," she said as if she hadn't made him wait several seconds for her answer. "I'm sure you've made some very effective changes."

He stalked her around the chair, forcing her to move and place it between them once more. Her hip bumped the mahogany table. She set her glass of juice down before she spilled it.

"You didn't meet Harrison today. He's in the Midwest right now. He's our CFO."

"That's nice." She couldn't see what possible concern it was of hers.

"He's retiring in September." He rolled the chair back and moved in on her position at the head of the table.

Her pulse rate rose. Heat flushed her skin. Her fingers tingled. It could have been his closeness. Or, it could have been presentiment for the words about to come out of his mouth.

She didn't say anything. He raised his hand to trail a finger down her cheek. Fire followed his touch. A swell of moisture started deep inside her.

Did her body anticipate his hand on her breast, beneath her skirt? Or was it the hot certainty that he was going to offer her a job?

A finger delved beneath the strap of her sundress, stroking rhythmically. "CFO. Isn't that your goal?"

She had the urge to wrench his hand from her shoulder. But that might make him think he bothered her. "I'll *earn* my CFO stripes. I don't need them handed to me."

Unfazed by the caustic tone, he let his fingers glide down to follow the scooped neckline. Her nipples tightened. She didn't bother to try to hide either that or the slight shudder that rippled through her.

Nor did she avoid his intense gaze as he whispered seductively. "I'm not handing it to you. I'm offering it."

"In exchange for what? An exquisite fuck?" She hoped to anger him by using his Friday-night phrasing.

It didn't work. He smiled wickedly. "While fucking you is exquisite, I would never stoop to sexual harassment. I'm offering because you have the appropriate background and knowledge of our unique business."

"And how would you know that?"

"Walter said you practically grew up in the winery."

Now that shocked her. Her father had always seemed irritated that she was underfoot. It hadn't stopped her, though. She'd found ways to sneak in, but … she hadn't imagined he'd tell his stepson and CEO about it.

"That was years ago," she answered

He turned both palms to her, cupping her breasts. She tried to step back, then realized he'd pinned her against the conference table. In circular motion, he gently caressed her, the peaks of her nipples beading urgently against the center of his palms. She had the insane urge to shove the length of her body against his, to jam his hands hard on her breasts.

"But you want it, don't you?"

God, yes, she wanted it. Right here, right now. Regardless of how angry, jealous or bitter she felt about everything else to do with the man, she still wanted his hands on her and his penis inside her. She was a willing victim of sexual desire. Her body remembered last night's implosion and craved more.

"The job, I mean," he amended, fooling neither of them.

His erection rubbed her abdomen. Her body, with a will of its own, rubbed back. His masterful hands maneuvered down her sides, squeezed her buttocks, then began manipulating the hem of her dress upward.

"I already have a job."

"A mere controller," he scoffed, licking her ear. She shivered.

"But there's so much room to grow there." She jolted beneath the heat of his touch as he found her bare thighs and stroked her skin.

"And exactly what do you want to grow into?" He stepped back then and turned her facing away, bending her to place her hands flush against the tabletop. He arched into her, his rigid cock finding solace in a thrust between her butt cheeks.

She tried to remember if he'd locked the door. "Well, there's always CEO, you know."

"As you might recall from our first conversation, I've got designs on the Chairman's seat. CEO will eventually be a vacant *position*." He leaned over her and humped her backside, just so there was no mistaking his meaning.

"Chairman of the Board is my father's job."

"He and my mother want to travel. He'll be stepping down so he can enjoy life a little more. And for his health."

Both his hands found their way to her inner thighs. His thumbs skimmed perilously close to her thinly covered mound.

"And I won't let you seduce me in his boardroom," she said half-heartedly. She desperately wanted to find out if he could surpass last night.

"No one's seducing anyone. We're negotiating." And he negotiated beneath the elastic of her thong panty, tangling his fingers in her curls in search of her entrance.

She kept her legs clamped firmly together, though that somehow added to the stimulation. "You couldn't make the offer sweet enough to get me back here for good."

This was stupid, she knew it. She was thinking with her clitoris instead of her brain. But, oh God, she wanted the burning flame of his touch on her.

He jammed a knee between her legs, forcing them apart, and slid two fingers deep inside her already soaked passage. She gasped, her body clenching around the delightful intrusion.

"There's sweet. And then there's the irresistible," he said against her nape. "I think I've got exactly the right bribe that'll make you take the job."

His thumb found her clitoris, just the way she wanted. The digit swirled in her juices. She shuddered and rocked back against him, trapping his hand and working it harder against her.

"Are you talking about benefits here?"

"Yeah. Our package is better than anything you'll find back in Silicon Valley." One hand fumbled between them, his belt buckle jingled, his zipper rasped. Then the naked pulsing ridge of his cock nudged her.

"I'm sure the package is impressive."

He tugged her panties down, guiding her to step out with first one foot, then the other. "Why don't we take the chairman's seat, and I'll lay out the details of the whole plan?"

Twisting her in his arms, he sat in the leather executive chair, then pulled her down on top of him. She grabbed the lapels of his jacket to steady herself.

Then she met his burning gaze.

"First of all," he said. "We pride ourselves in protecting all our employees." He produced a condom from the inner pocket of his jacket. "Put it on for me."

"That's not one of my skills."

"We provide on-the-job-training."

"All right. Let me get as far as I can on my own. Then you can tell me how to complete the task."

She slid back on his knees, then planted her feet on the floor, making sure she was steady before she stood. Her legs seemed to have the consistency of jelly. She parted his knees, pulled his pants and briefs to his ankles, then went down before him. She ripped the packet open with her teeth the way he'd done the other night.

"It's a very delicate operation," she said, taking his enormous cock in one hand.

She stroked, once up, once down. His breath hissed out.

"In addition, it's a very delicate instrument," he cautioned. "If you're not careful, it could explode in your fist."

"Does worker's comp cover that?"

"We'll have to check company policy. In the meantime, rest assured that if there are any mishaps, the company will make sure you're taken care of properly."

"Now, let me see, I think the next step would be to moisten the head of the instrument." She bent to take him in her mouth, sucking the crown, then grazing it with her teeth.

Again, he sucked in air. "I must caution you again about the highly explosive nature."

She stuck her tongue in the slit, felt his shudder, then relented. "All right. I'll begin the protection process. As I recall, I leave a small reservoir at the tip, then I slide down the latex covering, very slowly, gripping the tool tightly in my hand, careful not to jerk it off."

He rewarded her with a groan. "An excellent job, Miss Jarreau. The results will become a permanent record in your personnel file."

She gazed up at him through barely open eyes. God, he made her hot. Her made her want to come, to make *him* come.

He made her wonder how she was going to leave this afternoon. Except that there was the promise of next weekend.

But next weekend was for her father.

"I can see you're thinking too hard, Miss Jarreau. If you don't want a demerit going on your record, you'll approach your worktable right now." He patted his knees.

She climbed over him, fit her knees down between the arms of the chair and his flanks. "Are we still discussing benefits or is this another aptitude test?"

"Let's talk about benefits. The first benefit is the tight fit you'll find with this firm." He raised her hips and tugged her close, centering her over his stiff cock. "Put it in," he whispered.

She pumped him in her fist, then spread her labia and eased him just inside her channel. He joined his hand with hers and moistened his finger, then flicked the button of her clitoris.

"And then, of course," he continued, "there's the hands-on approach we like here at Jarreau Wineries." He manipulated her. Her hips undulated against his touch, drawing him deeper.

"In addition to the requisite medical, dental and vision insurance, we like to ensure that our employees are completely satisfied. Our satisfaction is dependent on theirs, you see. Take more," he urged.

She did, taking all of him in a sudden plunge. His eyes closed. "Aaah," slipped from his lips, then, "We strive for mutual satisfaction."

She rode him, her slick passage milking him.

"We also like to provide new challenges for our employees, new experiences." One hand still worked her clitoris; the other slipped past her hip to her rear cleft. He moistened his finger with her juices, then eased back the scant distance to her rear entrance.

He nudged the opening. Her movements stopped, and her eyes flew open to meet his.

"Sometimes our employees are reluctant. In that situation, we take it slowly."

She swallowed, her throat suddenly dry. No man had ever touched her that way.

"And we never force our employees to take more than they can handle." He eased the tip of his finger inside, all the while working her clitoris. She felt immensely filled. She wanted more. With his urging, she began to rock once more on his cock.

"That's it, baby, take me in, all of me."

As she moved, his finger slipped higher. It didn't hurt. In fact, with the combined effort of all his digits, she felt … overwhelmed.

"Does that feel good?"

"Oh God," she said. She started to pant. Everything he did felt so good. Everything about him felt so right.

She shuddered as much with a sudden gush of fear as she did with sexual ecstasy.

He touched a spot in her that caused her to shudder, that made her body flood with cream. She suddenly felt as if every nerve ending was on fire. Bright bolts of lightning seemed to burst before her eyes. She grabbed his shoulders, pumping him, impaling herself on his cock and his finger.

"Oh my God, oh my God," she chanted.

She didn't feel the orgasm build, didn't even need to strain for it—it was just there, rolling over her like a tidal wave. Stealing her breath. Suffocating her. She was barely aware of his mouth clamping down on hers, his hands guiding her hips, his cock jamming into her now.

They swallowed each others' cries. She bit his lip. He trapped her chin and ate at her mouth. Their breath came in gasps and pants. And she was sure it was hours that she lay collapsed on his lap before she could breathe normally again.

"You did lock the door, didn't you? " she murmured into his shirt collar.

"No. Didn't you?"

She reared back to find him laughing at her. She hated to be laughed at.

"Just kidding," he said. "Of course, I locked it."

"You locked the door when we first came in?"

"Right. I always think ahead."

"And you thought far enough ahead to bring a condom?"

He grinned. "I was a boy scout when I was kid. We always come prepared."

"Which means you planned this?"

He flexed his penis inside her. "Boy scouts aim to please, ma'am."

She stared at him. He'd had sex with her that first night, then he'd tried to shame her into coming home. She would have anyway. Now, he wanted to bribe her with a job and an orgasm.

So what if she'd succumbed readily enough?

She didn't have to voice her thoughts. Only an idiot would have missed her nonverbal clues. And Len Falconer, whatever else he might be, was no idiot.

"Don't say you didn't like it, especially my finger up your ass."

"You're vulgar." But she was still mortified. How could she have let him do that? Worse, how could she actually have liked it?

She jerked off his lap and hunted for her panties. Seconds later, she stepped into them, pulled them to her hips, then smoothed her dress into place.

"So, do you want the job?"

He was an insufferable pig. "No."

He stood, pulled his pants to his waist, tucked, zipped, and belted himself. He didn't, however, dispose of the condom. Probably not something he wanted to leave in the boardroom waste basket.

"Justine, do we have to start with the cold shoulder all over again?"

Change the earlier epithet to arrogant asshole. "No." She gave him her sweetest smile, the one reserved for idiotic bank tellers who had *her* money and no desire to fork it over without a hassle. "I loved every moment of it. And yes." She tapped a finger against her lip. "I do believe it was better than last night." She narrowed her gaze at him. "Now, can you please take me back to the house so I can collect my bag and my car?"

"You're not leaving."

"Did I hear a question mark at the end of that sentence?"

He stared at her for a long moment, then shook his head. "Whatever the employee wants." She felt the sting of his sarcasm. "I'll just use the executive washroom first."

Jarreau's had never had an executive washroom before.

But then Jarreau Wineries now belonged to the Falconers.

CHAPTER FIFTEEN

It had been the most incredible fuck of his life. He'd never before realized how sexy banter and the possibility of discovery could enhance the sex act. But what he'd just experienced had been more than sex. True, he'd planned the interlude. He'd brought the condoms, and he'd locked the door. But it had morphed into something more than mere sex. It bore the unmistakable earmark of an epiphany.

He'd planned her seduction, but he'd been the one seduced. As the last drop of come pulsed from him, he'd felt oddly … complete. At peace. Content. With her in his arms. He'd almost wanted to keep her there forever.

So, what the hell was wrong with *her*? She'd wanted it as much as he had. She'd shot heavenward like a missile. And exactly six seconds later, she'd shown her she-claws. Hadn't what they shared meant anything to her?

He stopped. And then he laughed out loud. For Christ's sake, he sounded like a woman.

"What?" she said, still staring straight ahead through the windshield.

He didn't enlighten her.

But he'd sure as hell enlightened himself.

Somehow, he'd overlooked his growing attachment. He'd labeled his emotions as being born of loyalty to the newest member of his family. He'd called it a one-night-stand. He'd written off his pursuit as the single-minded goal of repaying Walter.

Justine was more than the sum of her actions. She'd left her father, but who the hell was he to judge the reasons why? She hadn't hesitated to return when she'd learned of her father's illness; her bag had been packed when he'd arrived Saturday morning. As for going back to her job, he admired a woman with a sense of responsibility, and he understood her dilemma.

There could be no doubt about it any longer. He wanted Justine for more than a night. One night, one weekend, one month, even one year, wasn't enough. Christ, he might actually want a lifetime. He'd have to marry her to get that.

Right now, he was pretty damn sure Justine wouldn't take him for any length of time.

And he really did sound just like a woman. Overthinking and overanalyzing the entire situation.

"Ha." He chuckled.

"You're really starting to freak me out. What are you thinking?"

He smiled in the face of her glower. "Something totally diabolical. I'll tell you about it later." After he'd come up with a plan to get her to marry him.

He turned, following the gently curving driveway around to the front of the house. His heart started to pound. Roman's car sat at the bottom of the flagstone steps. He glanced at Justine, but, of course, she had no idea who it belonged to. He parked behind the silver sedan. His temple throbbed like a drumbeat.

She didn't wait for him to come round the hood to open her door.

The house was ominously silent as they entered. He fought the urge to take the stairs several steps at a time. Instead he clenched his fists. A knuckle cracked in the quiet.

"What's wrong?" she whispered, picking up on the subtle tension flowing through his body.

He debated telling her anything at all until he knew the worst. But she'd find out soon enough. "Roman's here."

"Roman?"

"Your father's doctor."

"Oh shit." The color fled from her cheeks as if she'd seen a ghost.

"I'll check on him. You'll wait here?" He ended the sentence on a slightly higher note, making it a question instead of an edict. He touched her hand to discover cold fingers.

She shuddered in his grip.

"Yes, I'll wait here."

~

It was strictly cowardice. She should be rushing to follow Len up the wide, winding stairway.

But she didn't want to see her father gasping for breath or clutching his chest, or worse, unconscious and as white as the sheets he lay on. She'd never seen a heart attack; she'd never seen a dead person.

She didn't want her father to be the first for either.

Len was gone for long minutes. She sat on the bottom step, facing the front door and clasped her hands until they hurt. She strained for every sound as if that would tell her what was happening. Which was stupid; all she had to do was climb those stairs.

Now I lay me down to sleep ...

That was the extent of the prayers she knew.

Please don't let him be dead.

Please don't let him be dying.

God, she'd had sex while her father lay dying. She'd had a petty argument with her stepbrother. She'd contemplated her trip home, the long hours in the car, the myriad of silly, inane tasks she'd have to accomplish at work tomorrow.

As intently as she thought she'd been listening, she didn't hear Len's approach. She didn't even realize he'd returned until he sat down beside her and pried one of her hands from the other where they'd lain stiffly in her lap.

His hands were warm. Warm hands, cold heart. No, it was the other way round, cold hands, warm heart.

She stared at the pattern in the parquet. "He's all right, isn't he?"

"Roman said he'll be fine. It was a mild attack."

"Another one?"

"A little while after we left."

She sucked in a breath. "This morning I told him I had to leave. He was upset."

Len squeezed her fingers in his. "It wasn't your fault, Justine."

"But I should have—"

He put a finger to her lips. "You did everything you were supposed to, everything you possibly could."

She looked at him, his visage slightly blurred at the edges. "Why are you being so nice to me?"

He stroked the tips of her fingers where they poked from his grasp. "Contrary to the way I've acted, I don't really believe you're a heartless bitch. I know you're worried about him as much as anyone."

She rolled her lips between her teeth and bit down hard. The sheer compassion in his words melted her heart and made her eyes water.

"Roman's still checking him out. You can go up and see him when Roman leaves, if you'd like."

She wiped at a tiny bit of moisture that had leaked from the corner of her eye. "Okay. I have to make a phone call first anyway."

He stood and pulled her to her feet, staring down at her with ... well, she wasn't sure what it was. But it made her heart beat faster with more than just fear for her father.

"You can use the phone in the office." He gave her a little shove in that direction.

She thrust down her confusion and made her way into the office and to her father's desk. The scent of leather and Len's musky cologne filled her head. Not her father's desk, then, Len's. She sat in the worn leather chair and felt as if his warmth enveloped her.

She picked up the phone to dial.

The "dickhead" had to be paged.

"I trust you're on your way home, Justine," were the first words out of his dickhead mouth.

She gulped a deep breath to calm herself. "No, I'm not."

The line vibrated with his exasperated exhalation. "Justine, no one can understand what you did with the currency conversions on the German consolidation."

"I went through the whole thing step-by-step last time with Morten. Tell him to go back to the work papers and read his documentation."

"Don't use that tone with me, Justine."

She tucked the receiver between her ear and shoulder, then laced her fingers together. What she'd really like to do was pound the instrument against the desk and make the man's ears explode.

"Mr. Freidman, please tell Morten he can call me anytime to discuss the consolidation. Here's the number." She rattled off the home extension.

"It would be preferable if you were here tomorrow when the auditors get in."

She continued with excessive politeness. "My father's had another attack, Mr. Freidman. I'm not sure when I can get in. But you, or anyone who has a question, can call me. I can talk you through whatever it is." Not likely if it was her boss. The man was as dense as a fence post.

"That simply won't do."

She began to feel light-headed with all the deep, calming breaths he forced her to take. "There is no alternative."

"I'm afraid that I find your sense of duty sadly lacking."

"My sense of duty is to my family, Mr. Freidman. Work comes second, as it should for everyone."

"You leave me no choice, Justine. If you are not here tomorrow morning when I get in, don't bother coming back at all."

"Are you firing me?"

"I will tomorrow. Your final check can be couriered to your home."

"You can't do that. What about Family Leave?"

"We're in a crisis situation here. And you're letting the ship sink."

With the "dickhead" at the helm, the ship was bound to sink anyway. The man *was* the goddamn iceberg in the way. She could have told him exactly what she thought of him, what *everyone* else thought of him, too.

Instead, Justine said, "That's fine, Mr. Freidman. Fire me. Because I won't be there tomorrow morning. You can send my check to my apartment, but make sure it doesn't require a signature, and it'll fit in my mailbox. And please tell Morten I'd be more than happy to answer any of his questions if he'd like to call me down here."

"You're fired, and I'm not paying you for any questions you answer," he screeched.

She kept talking as if he hadn't opened his mouth. "And I'll be by to clean out my desk when my father is out of danger."

She hung up amidst a flurry of invectives. Then she muttered one of her own. "Dillhole."

She shivered all the way down to her toes. She'd just committed herself to staying.

~

My sense of duty is to my family. Work comes second, as it should for everyone.

She hadn't said that for his benefit. She hadn't even known that he'd leaned against the paneling outside the office unabashedly eavesdropping.

Dillhole. He smiled to himself. It wasn't an epithet he expected Justine to know. Yet it described her boss quite effectively, even if he had only heard Justine's half of the conversation.

The dillhole had fired her. She'd taken it with equanimity.

This was exactly what Walter needed. The strain on the old man's heart would be relieved as soon as he heard that Justine was staying. For good.

This time, he took the stairs two at a time with far less heavy a heart.

CHAPTER SIXTEEN

Walter beamed and yanked himself straight up against the pillows. "Damn, Len, I knew you could do it."

"It wasn't me. It was your second attack."

"You charmed her, Len, admit it."

"She really didn't need charming, Walter." She'd made the decision to stay on her own. *My sense of duty is to my family.* Even now, he felt a certain sense of pride in her.

Roman refilled his little black doctor's bag with a variety of instrumentation. "And while you're both busy congratulating yourselves, you can also thank Naomi for putting up with your antics."

His mother had retired to her room. Which was strange, now that he thought about it.

Walter began to glower. "Roman."

Len let his gaze drift from one to the other, watching the silent communication furrow Walter's brow and produce a frown on Roman's lips.

"What's going on, Doctor?"

Roman snapped his case shut, picked it up, then let it hang at his side. "I refuse to be a part of family squabbles. Len, your stepfather's fine. He needs less red meat, less stress, more playtime with your mother, but otherwise he's fine." He turned to his old friend. "And you," he pointed his finger, "You need to apologize to your wife, even if you have to get down on your hands and knees to beg her forgiveness. Personally, I think she ought to hold out a few weeks just to make you sweat. Except then I really might have to put you in the hospital."

With that incomprehensible diatribe, he marched from the room.

"What the hell was he talking about, Walter?"

Walter grimaced, waved his arms around and groused. "He's just an old woman. I think I need a new doctor. He's lost his knack."

"And you're lying."

Walter stopped dead, then began to sputter. "I'm your Chairman. You can't talk to me that way."

Len clenched his teeth. "Then tell me what Roman was talking about."

"I told you—"

"You faked the whole thing to get Justine to come home, didn't you?"

"Don't be ridiculous." Walter glowered and met his gaze head-on.

But while Walter was an excellent poker player, Len now had the advantage. He knew when he was being bluffed. Shit, he should have known right from the beginning.

"The first heart attack was real, sweetheart." His mother stood just inside the door. He hadn't heard it open. "It was a wake-up call. But I can't let Walter take all the blame for this. I went along with letting him exaggerate the situation."

"I don't believe this." He felt like pounding his fist against something.

She bent her head. "I'm ashamed. It was wrong."

"Mother, how the hell could you let us all think he was dying?"

"I could say that I kept assuring you he wasn't. But I intentionally let body language and long periods of brooding give you the impression I wasn't telling the truth."

"You're a helluvan actress, Mother. I didn't know you had it in you. I think you might even be better than Walter here. Why did you lie at all?"

"It wasn't her fault, Len. It wasn't even her idea. I just thought it was the only way to get Justine back."

"Tell him the truth, Walter. I'm tired of lying."

He raised an eyebrow. "There's more?"

"Well, there's—"

"Naomi, you're going to get it all wrong."

"How can you get the truth wrong, Walter?"

Len held up a hand. "Stop. This had a beginning, it had a middle, and I'm calling an end to it. Now, did you have a heart attack last week?

"Well, son, it's like this—"

"That wasn't an open-ended question, Walter. It requires only a yes or no answer."

"Yes, he had a heart attack," his mother replied.

"Did you have a heart attack today?"

Walter sighed. "No, I didn't."

"And when I was up here before and you told me you had … why?"

"It's like I tried to tell—"

Len growled low in his throat. Sonuvabitch.

"I wanted Justine to come home."

His mother glided to his side. "And we wanted you two to get to know each other, because we thought you'd be perfect for each other."

"You were match-making?" He'd heard it all now. He just couldn't believe it.

"But most of all, I wanted Justine back." Walter stretched out a hand, then let it fall back to the bed. "I had the heart attack, and it made me realize that anything could happen."

"Couldn't you have just picked up the phone and called her? That would have been easier."

"What if she'd said no?"

It hit Len then like a two-by-four. Walter was afraid. Not of dying. He was afraid of Justine's rejection. The man had been CEO of Jarreau Wineries for some fifty-odd years. But he was afraid his own daughter wouldn't forgive him.

"Why don't you tell me why she really left fifteen years ago." It wasn't a question; it was a demand. He knew damn well he'd never heard the whole story. Maybe he'd never even heard part of it.

"Yes, *Daddy*, why don't you tell us all why I left? I'm wondering if you even remember."

Justine spoke from the doorway, a brittle edge of anger in her voice.

"Justine." Walter's anguished tones told the story.

"That's my name, all right. Good, you're remembering. Why don't you tell us the rest of the tale?"

She was gorgeous in her outrage. It made him incredibly hot despite his own ire. Or, maybe because of it. She was spoiling for a fight. And she deserved to get it. He stepped back to let her have her well-earned due.

"Give it up, Walter," his mother encouraged. "There's no use fighting it anymore.

Justine vibrated with her anger. Walter had never given up on a fight in his life. He'd always had to win. It wasn't simply a habit he had learned in the five years Len had known him.

"It was over a man," Walter said.

She snorted. "Is that what you really believe?"

"George would have been good for you, Justine. He would have taken care of you."

Interesting. The man they'd quarreled over hadn't been of Justine's choosing. Nor had Justine left her father to be with him, she'd left because she *didn't* want him. That fact put an entirely different spin on things.

"I didn't need to be taken care of," she went on vehemently. "And I think I've proven that, since I've done extremely well since you cut me off. I own my own flat in San Francisco. I've got a good job." At least she had until today, Len realized, because she'd bought into Walter's lies.

"I make a good salary," she added. "I'm going places."

"I didn't cut you off."

Trust Walter to ignore everything else she said but that. "You refused to pay for the remainder of my college education. You refused to give me living expenses. You refused to help me at all unless I came home and married George. I'd call that cutting me off."

He wondered how hard that must have been, remembering her penchant for doggie bags.

"I just thought it would be best if you didn't finish college. What did you really need it for anyway?"

Walter must have missed the sixties and the rise of feminism.

"I needed it so I didn't have to be dependent on some *man* for the rest of my life." Every bit of anger and bitterness she had felt went into that one word.

"But I'd have taken care of you no matter what," Walter beseeched.

Len didn't have an ounce of sympathy for him.

Neither, it seemed, did Justine. "I never wanted to be taken care of. I just wanted to be an integral part of the winery."

Walter sighed and shook his head. "Honey, women can't be CEOs. It's just not in their temperament. It's a jungle out there, and men were raised to fight in that jungle."

Len couldn't help himself—he laughed outright. "Guess you haven't read Fortune Magazine lately, Walter? I must loan you my latest copy. There's quite an interesting article on several high-powered female executives."

"But they're hard, Len. Callused. They're toughened like men. They even dress like men."

He should have remained pissed the geezer had lied to him. Instead he suddenly felt sorry for Walter, for that all-important relationship the old man had thrown away heedlessly.

He looked at Justine, all ultra-feminine and ultra-sexy. And she'd just, albeit politely and diplomatically, told her boss to go fuck himself when he'd acted the … dillhole. She wasn't a woman who'd back down in a fight.

He admired that in her. He more than admired her. And he'd made the biggest fucking mistake buying into Walter's garbage. He intended telling her he'd misjudged her badly the moment he got her alone.

"Aren't you being overly dramatic, Walter?" he asked mildly

Justine turned the full force of her glare on him. "I don't need your help. And who are you to talk anyway? You're as bad as him."

Whoa. She'd sure as hell gotten her dander up. Not that he could blame her. Walter had abused her. He held up his hands in surrender.

Once more she went on the offensive with her father. "You should have given me a chance. You should have believed in me. You should even have called me to say you were getting married." Resentment shone in her eyes. "But the one thing you should never have done was lie to me about your heart attack. I could have forgiven everything else. But not that."

"But honey—"

She held up her hand. "Don't say another word. It'll only be another lie or a bribe or some form of manipulation designed to get me to stay on *your* terms. I'm not staying. I'm not selling my flat."

"But, Justine—"

"Good-bye, Father. Have a nice life."

Nice exit line. She didn't slam the door, but closed it quietly and unobtrusively. The snick of the latch falling home boomed in the silent bedroom.

His mother patted Walter's hand. "Len will talk to her, sweetheart. It'll work out. She'll understand."

"I'm not talking to her on his behalf, Mother. I've got my own shit to explain." He turned to Walter. "And maybe you need to get down on your hands and knees and beg her to forgive you. I know that's what I'm going to do."

With that, he left the room and charged down the hall. Justine wasn't leaving this goddamn house until she'd heard him out.

CHAPTER SEVENTEEN

"You're not listening to me, Justine." He tore off his suit jacket and threw it across the chair in the corner of her room.

"I heard every word you said," she answered as she continued tossing her stuff into the bag she'd laid open across the footstool at the end of the bed. "You're sorry that you believed my father's story about why I left. You're sorry that you said such awful things to me when we first met. You want me to stay and be your CFO. And you love me."

She recited it all with the enthusiasm allotted a grocery list.

"Yes, goddamn it, I'm in love you."

She folded a pair of jeans, then tossed them in the case, ignoring the fact that they'd landed askew. "I have a job. I have a home. I'm not giving any of that up."

"You don't have a job to go back to. You got fired, remember?"

She raised her eyes to glare at him for exactly two seconds, then returned to her haphazard packing. "I don't like being eavesdropped on, either."

"Okay, I'm sorry about that, too."

"Apology accepted. In fact, I accept all your apologies. But I'm still going back to San Francisco."

"To work for—what's his name? Dillhole Freidman? With that ass for a boss, you'll be looking for another job within six months, I guarantee it."

"At least I'll make sure I don't work for a lying, cheating, manipulative SOB when I go job hunting."

"I never cheated."

She smiled. "I haven't known you long enough for that to happen." Then she flung in a few tantalizingly skimpy thongs and a lacy bra

Jesus. He hadn't gotten a chance to get her out of that one. He'd have used his teeth to edge the lace aside, then his tongue to—"Goddamn it! Stop packing and listen to me."

She very deliberately set her cosmetics bag inside the case, then crossed her arms over her chest. "I've been listening. I just haven't heard anything that makes me want to stay."

That cut deep. A declaration of love wasn't enough for her. She wanted some groveling. Well, he wasn't a man who groveled.

There were other things he was *much* better at.

He closed the distance between them in less than a second, never even giving her the chance to get away from him. "I love you. And I'll prove you love me."

He trailed a finger down her cheek, across her lips, down her throat, lingering in the hollow there, then on to the swell of a plump, luscious breast. Her nipple peaked. He thumbed the bud.

"Case in point," he whispered, pinching gently.

She shuddered. "I never said I didn't like fucking you. I'm not a liar like some people we know."

"I never lied."

"Oh yeah. I forgot. You're a man. And you buy into the Clintonian definition that omission of crucial details isn't a lie."

He bent to the sweet, scented skin of her neck, sucked up some flesh, then bit down lightly.

She sighed, her breath hitching just before she actually allowed him to hear a moan. He smiled against her throat. He was winning, he knew it. He'd open her mind just like he'd open her legs. He'd get her to accept what they both felt when he got her to accept his body inside hers.

"And it's not fucking," he muttered just before he stuck his tongue in the hollow at the base of her throat. "It's making love."

Her caustic laugh turned into a gasp as he put his hand between her legs and rubbed her through her already damp silk panties.

"See, you want it, baby. I can give it to you. Whatever you want, any way you want."

~

Frigid anger stole through her like a cold wintry thing. Her teeth chattered, her arms trembled, and her belly shivered with it. It dulled the edges of her vision and forced her to concentrate for every breath.

God, the man would stop at nothing. He'd tried every trick in the book to bend her to his will. He'd lied about her father's condition. He'd manipulated her with sex. He'd bribed her with the job she'd always wanted—well, not exactly, because she'd always wanted to be CEO, and that job, she knew, he would never give up unless he got to be Chairman first. When none of those tricks worked, he decided to tell her he loved her.

It would have hurt if she'd hadn't been riding her anger like a knife blade, the edge so sharp that it sliced without pain.

Filthy, dirty, rotten, lowlife bastard. No offense to Naomi. Then again, Naomi had raised him. She'd helped create a man who was as manipulative and sneaky as Justine's own father.

Payback time. Len wanted to seduce her. She'd let him. She'd take as many of those lovely orgasms—because he really was very good at it—as he wished to dispense. Then she'd walk out the door and slam it in his face.

"Aren't you even going to ask me what *I* want?"

He eased back from her, but continued to stroke her through the panties. God, she could come from that alone. And she'd certainly miss it when she left.

But that's what vibrators were for.

"What do you want me to do?" His pupils were huge, the color of his eyes that deep, dark shade of semi-sweet chocolate she found so tempting.

"Kiss me. You never kiss me enough." And she loved kissing, the lips, the tongue and the little bites. When she was alone with her vibrator, she would remember it all.

And she could put another man's face to the fantasy.

Abandoning the massage between her legs, he used both hands to cup her face. His tongue glided over her lips, mimicking the stroke he'd used so effectively on her clitoris. He tasted so damn good, like the finest of wines, the sweetest of grapes. He sucked, stroked and teased, then used his tongue along the seam to ease her lips open. She accepted him. Her arms went around his neck, and she strained on her toes to get as much as she could. He gave a beautiful kiss, just the right amount of moisture and tension and tongue.

It was surely something she could teach someone else. Men were like dogs, they could be trained.

"What else do you want?"

Drifting somewhere between heaven and hell, she almost didn't notice that he'd backed off and spoken between nibbles.

What else? She liked fucking, down-and-dirty stuff. Yes, she did. But she also liked to be pampered.

And she'd take everything he offered and feel no obligation to give anything in return.

"Kiss my back. Lick it all over." Most men never took the time to do her back justice. That entire expanse of flesh was even more an erogenous zone than her breasts.

Len turned her, nudging her around the end of the footstool until her knees hit the edge of the bed. "You should have told me you wanted attention back there."

He should have goddamn known, selfish asshole.

Easing her zipper open, he kissed every inch of flesh he exposed. The spaghetti straps of her dress slid down her arms. He guided her to step out of it, after which he pushed her forward onto the bed.

He came down on top of her. He started with the top of her spine, working his way down until he reached the cleft of her buttocks. She squirmed and writhed beneath him. More than anything, she wanted the touch of his finger between her legs, on her clitoris. And she'd be off like a rocket, straight to the moon or Mars.

Except that would be too easy on him.

But Len wasn't done. He bracketed her with his hands, smoothing them along her sides, fleetingly slipping beneath her to tease her nipples. An unbelievable combination of sensation. He left not one square inch unexplored, using his mouth, his tongue and his teeth. His beard-roughed chin scraped her skin, leaving a tingling in its wake.

Her fingers clutched at the bedspread. She moaned and twisted and bit her lip to trap a full-throated cry inside. Ask and you shall receive. Oh my God. Could she live without this? Of course, she could. All she had to do was remember. Then let her own fingers do the walking. She didn't need *him*.

He traced the upper edge of her thong panty, slipping a finger beneath the elastic. He leaned over to nip her buttock.

Please fuck me, please fuck me.

"What do you want now? Tell me. Anything."

She wondered if she'd chanted aloud. But no, he wanted to control her by answering her every request. Only *she* was the one in control. And she wanted him battered and hurting and down. Too bad he lied about being in love with her.

"Eat me."

He rolled her over, stripped her panties off and pitched them across the room. "My pleasure."

He buried his head between her legs. She almost cried out at his first touch. Snarling, her fingers in his hair, she pulled on the locks until she thought his scalp might scream. He never broke contact.

Yes, oh God. Yes, just like that.

His tongue drove her almost to the edge, then he softened the assault, sucking gently. He wedged his hand between them and entered her with two fingers. She wrapped her legs around his shoulders and held on as he rocked against her, his fingers inside her. Then he hit her full bore once again, driving his tongue against her clitoris. Her womb ached for release, and her hips moved in perfect tandem to the stroke of his tongue. She tossed her head side-to-side on the bedspread, her hair covering her face, sticking to her lips. Her back arched off the bed, and she allowed herself a deep moan that seemed to travel the length of her body. She dug her heels into his back.

"Make me come, please make me come. Oh please."

She started to pant and relished the final climb to the edge of climax. Then orgasm cascaded over her. Her hips bucked, and he clung to her buttocks, melding his mouth to her sex.

It was so damn good it hurt.

She became aware of his quickened breath, his quaking muscles when she hit bottom again. Rising on her elbows, she looked at him still lying between her legs.

Triumph gleamed in his eyes.

"Ask me for more," he whispered throatily.

He didn't even see defeat coming.

CHAPTER EIGHTEEN

"Fuck me," Justine murmured.

"Where are the condoms?"

Several packets remained in her nightstand. Exhausted, she could only point. He tore off his tie and shirt, kicked off his shoes without untying them, then dropped his pants and boxers on the floor. Climbing back on the bed, he crawled over her to reach the drawer. Male musk and the spice of her own juices filled her nostrils like perfume. The ridge of his cock jabbed her belly as he moved. Anticipating his entry, her body oozed cream.

He made fast work of the condom, then held out his arms. "Come here, baby. I think I'm going to die if I don't get inside you."

She wanted to smack that "baby" shit right off his face. But worse, she wanted him deep inside her. She scrambled across the bed to where he'd sprawled.

"How do you want it, baby?"

"On top."

"Jesus, yes. You are so good to me."

She'd be good all right. Then she'd slam him down.

She spread her legs over his haunches, took his cock in her hand, then impaled herself. A long, slow sigh fell from her lips as he filled her. He was right. It was good.

He molded his hands to her hips, urging her movements.

"Christ. I'll never get enough of this. I'll never get enough of you."

He was right about that, too. Because this was the last time he'd get her at all.

She let her head fall back, closed her eyes, and concentrated on the rhythm and his deep thrusts. He put a slick finger to her little button as she rode him, massaged her as she pumped. Oh yes, he filled her exquisitely. She clenched her thighs and her vaginal muscles, working him, working herself.

She wanted to scream and scream and scream with the intolerable pleasure of it underlain as it was with an unbearable anger. Until somehow the two emotions became one. Colors burst over her; sensations burst within. She bit down on her lip, tasting blood and the remnants of his kiss. His body hurled upward against her. His fingers bruised her hips as he pounded himself to orgasm and her beyond the limits of her endurance.

She came then, not because she allowed it to happen, but because she couldn't stop herself. The room ceased to exist. The bed no longer seemed to hold her. There was just his body between her legs and his cock claiming ownership. She fell against him, chest to chest, crying his name and clutching his shoulders as she rode out the storm he alone created.

She came to her senses with a ringing in her ears and strange spots before her eyes. Her cheeks felt wet and her eyelashes gummy. Her chest ached as if her breath had been stolen from her for long minutes. She licked coppery blood from her lips, dragging in his scent along with much needed air.

His arms were wrapped fully, protectively, around her body.

"Christ." His breath soughed against her ear. "I love you."

A sudden chill raised goosebumps along her arms. He rubbed them away with long, warm strokes.

How the hell could she possibly match that storm of sensation on her own? Didn't matter. She'd have to make do.

"Did I scream?"

His laughter rumbled over her, ruffled the tangled strands of her hair. "We both did."

"Shit." She disengaged body parts, his penis exiting with an audible pop. She felt almost as if the action sucked something vital from her.

"Where are you going?"

She put one foot on the floor, then hitched the other leg over his body and stood. Legs wobbled, muscles twitched. Her dress and panties were on the other side of the bed. She padded round to get them.

"Justine?" Hands propped behind his head, penis semi-erect, condom intact, he watched her. And waited.

She stepped into the dress, reached behind for the zipper and pulled it up. Then came the thong. It strafed her oversensitive nerve endings. Suddenly, her body throbbed. Her chest hurt.

"Justine, what are you doing?"

She pulled a light cardigan sweater from her partially packed suitcase and pulled it over her shoulders. Air-conditioning. The drying perspiration had chilled her.

"I'm packing."

"But you're not leaving."

"Of course I am."

She moved to the bureau, pulled out another profusion of color, then tossed it in the bag.

~

Len lay like stone against the rumpled bedclothes. She'd drained every last drop of strength from him.

"You're going to leave after we made love like that?"

She pushed knotted locks of hair back from her forehead and looked at him. "Is that what that was?"

"You know damn well it was."

She arched an eyebrow. "Funny. I thought it was fucking. *Exquisite* fucking, I'll admit, but just fucking all the same."

He wanted to shake her. "That wasn't fucking."

She flipped her hair back. "Screwing, pumping, boinking. Call it whatever you like. It was still just casual, meaningless sex.

Her words burned a hole through him. "It was incredible. It's never been like that with anyone. Not for me." He swallowed. "Not for you either, I know."

She shrugged, then flapped the lid closed on her bag and zipped it. "Now I'll have something to strive for in my subsequent one-night-stands."

That galvanized him. He threw his legs over the side of the bed, stood, then stalked toward her. She was dressed; he was naked. Nudity had never before put him at a disadvantage.

She hefted her suitcase and set it on the floor.

"I meant it."

"What? That you love me?" She shrugged once more. "Probably." She jutted a hip and stuck her hand on it. "But I don't like your definition. It's selfish. It's manipulative. And it really isn't worth my time. You're a carbon copy of my father. You'll say and do anything to get what you want. And you don't give a damn if anyone gets hurt in the process. You'd have to look up the meaning of compromise in the dictionary. You say family comes first, but as far as I can tell, Len, you're the only who ever comes first."

133

"That's not true."

She tipped her head to one side. "Isn't it?"

He could have said he'd made sure she came first. Several times. But then he thought about the last four days. He thought about the things he'd done, and how he should have done them differently.

The answer was yes. He'd chosen to handle her the way Walter had always handled her. He hadn't lied, not exactly. But he'd planned on massaging her guilt to force her home. He'd used seduction to get her to stay. Then he'd resorted to blackmail or bribery or whatever the hell you called that job offer he'd made. He hadn't utilized lies, but then neither had he given her honesty.

Which was worse? The outright lie? Or the things he'd done to her?

"You're right," he said. "I was wrong. And I'm sorry."

"Yeah, I know." She lifted her bag. "But hey, thanks for a great fuck. For all of them, in fact. And tell your mom thanks for the hospitality."

Then she grabbed her purse off the bureau and left him.

CHAPTER NINETEEN

"You let her leave, Leonard."

Len stood at the window of his bedroom overlooking the long driveway Justine had vanished down not more than fifteen minutes ago.

"No one *lets* Justine do anything. She's got a mind of her own."

"Yes, but I thought ... well, we heard ... what I mean is ..." His mother simply couldn't describe what she'd heard.

But he could. She'd overheard him making delirious love to Justine. She'd overheard him crying out his passion for the most incredible woman he'd ever had the privilege of bringing to orgasm. She'd heard him trying to stamp an ownership label on Justine's ass.

She'd heard him making the biggest monumental mistake of his life.

Justine had been right. He had ruthlessly used the one thing he had to his advantage, her desire for him.

Operative word: used. No matter how else he tried to describe it, it all came down to that one fact. He'd *used*.

"Well, are you going after her?"

"I don't know what I'd say to her if I did." He didn't know how to do anything else but *use*. He was a man with an arsenal of weapons: intelligence, diplomacy, charisma, arrogance, and even his body. He had a knack for finding a person's weakness and exploiting it. But he'd always rationalized his actions. He never destroyed, he only employed techniques designed to promote growth, to guide those around him on to bigger and better things, according to his definition, of course.

And that was exactly what Walter had done when he'd driven Justine away fifteen years ago. The old man decided what was best for her, then he'd tried to force her to take it.

Len had gone to her room, intending to explain his actions and beg her forgiveness. But when she'd offered the slightest resistance, he'd reached amidst his weaponry and pulled out the one implement he'd thought would bring her around. Sex. Desire. Just another form of manipulation.

He always believed he knew what was best for everyone. Then he set about making sure they got it. But, like Walter, he had never bothered to ask what the person actually wanted.

He stroked his chin. "Do you think Darla likes Marketing?"

He felt his mother's worried gaze on him. "Of course, she does."

"But do you *know*?"

"Well, she wouldn't be doing it if she didn't like it."

"She seemed suited to it."

"And you wanted to find a place for her in the company."

"But is that what *she* wanted?"

"I …" She bit her lip. "I really don't know."

"I don't know about Brian, either."

"He seems happy. They both seem happy."

"*Seem*." He contemplated the rhododendrons lining the drive. A riot of color. To disguise the rot inside? "And what about you, Mom? Are you happy with Walter?"

"Len. It's not like you to be so …"

"To be so what, Mom? Questioning?"

"I was thinking more in terms of indecisive."

He laughed, although it came out more in the form of a self-deprecating snort. "I decided right up front that Walter'd be perfect for you."

"And you were right."

He stabbed his index finger to his chest. "Don't you get it? *I* don't have a right to decide. Not for any of you."

"Len, you're a leader. That's what leaders do, they lead. They make decisions. I wouldn't have you any other way."

And Justine wouldn't have him at all because of it. He didn't know how the hell to change her mind.

And maybe that was the crux of the whole thing. *He* couldn't change *her* mind.

He could only tell her that he loved her. That he'd do his best not to *lead* her.

And then he'd ask her what *she* wanted.

~

Justine had never used the word fuck so many times in her life as she had in the past four days. She'd passed the motionless oil pumps in San Ardo half an hour after leaving Len when she finally admitted to herself that she'd lied.

As a child she'd always imagined the pumps to be giant animals grazing on fragrant green grasses. They'd worked back then, their heads bobbing. She'd ignored the sulfur stink in the air and the haze that hung over the small valley from the nearby smoke stacks of the refineries. She'd always been a dreamer. She'd dreamed of being someone her father could be proud of. His captain of industry, his right-hand gal. She'd dreamed of creating a dynasty with her soul mate and raising a family of winemakers. She dreamed of passing on the heritage from generation to generation.

But at thirty-five, all she'd become was a liar. She'd lied to herself about where her anger lay. It wasn't with Len's machinations. It wasn't even with her father. It stemmed from her own broken dreams and from the fact that she'd actually lost the ability to dream somewhere along the way. CFO by the time she was forty. How the hell was she supposed to pass *that* on to future generations she hadn't even had the courage to start creating?

She worked so hard to build her career only to learn today—no, to remember—that she'd wanted far more. She should have realized that when she decided to go in search of that fatal one-night-stand. Something had been missing for a long time. She'd sought a patch instead of delving deep enough to find a cure.

She'd failed at relationships not because the men she dated wanted her to become some house frau, but because she'd been afraid they wouldn't value the things she had to offer. She was a coward.

And the worst was that she was too much of a coward to turn the car around and give Len the benefit of the doubt.

CHAPTER TWENTY

Justine left San Ardo behind, but not the confusing thoughts. They still wrenched her gut when she pulled off at the Burger King in King City. She used the facilities, washed her hands, splashed water on her pale face, and bought a carton of orange juice for a zap of energy.

She came out to find Len leaning against the front fender of her car, his arms crossed over his chest and dark sunglasses shielding his eyes from both the sun and her inspection.

"Hi," he said as she approached.

"Hello." She put a hand to her forehead to cut the glare of the sun.

God, he was heart-breakingly gorgeous. The late afternoon sun beat down on her back, but the heat which suffused through her came from more than a mere object that lived in the sky. Her skin still tingled at the remembered rasp of his beard. Her body moistened with the thrilling memory of his tongue. She could love this man if she could allow herself to believe in him.

He pulled off his sunglasses, folded them, then slid them in the pocket of his navy polo shirt. He squinted, fine lines reaching out from the corners of his eyes.

"Can we talk?"

She sucked on her juice straw to fill the sudden dryness of her mouth, then nodded.

He patted the fender beside him. "Will you come over here?"

She did, turning to sit beside him.

The scent of shower soap and shampoo evaporated off his skin. Justine was sure she still smelled of him, of their sex, their joined bodies. She never wanted to wash him off.

"I managed to catch up without getting a ticket."

"I wasn't driving all that fast." Less than the speed limit most of the time, the vehicular equivalent of dragging her feet.

"And I planned what I wanted to say."

Her chest tightened. "And what's that?"

"I wasn't satisfied with any of the things I came up with."

She closed her eyes, let the sun bathe her face, then she turned to look at him. "Want some of my orange juice?"

He took the carton she held out. His lips on the straw made her nipples pucker. He handed it back. "Thanks."

"Did you eat? We could have dinner inside."

"Are you trying to make it easier for me to grovel? Or, easier for you to let me down nicely?"

"Actually, I'm nervous. I was trying to make it easier for myself."

He reached over and picked up her hand, lacing his fingers through hers. "Then maybe I should just tell you why I followed you.

"Yeah."

"I would have gone all the way to San Francisco if I hadn't caught up with you on the way. But I have to admit, I saw myself as some road warrior, forcing you to pull off on the shoulder."

"Len." She tugged on his hand, her heart rat-a-tatting in her chest.

"Sorry. Guess I'm nervous, too."

He took a deep breath, and she believed him. Len Falconer, CEO and most likely soon-to-be chairman, was nervous.

She squeezed his hand.

"All right. Let me say first that I love you. I realize that you think I'm just trying to manipulate you into staying for your father's sake." He raised her hand to his mouth and licked a knuckle. "But right now I don't give a fuck about your father."

She opened her mouth to speak. He put a finger to her lips.

"Let me finish or I'll forget something."

"I thought you said you couldn't plan it out."

He gave her a look, and she wanted to crawl right inside him.

She zipped her lip with a flick of her wrist.

"I'm not sorry I made love to you, not today, not last Friday, not ever. I'm just sorry that I did it instead of telling you how I felt. And I should have *asked* how you felt. I knew you were angry, but I told myself it was all about your father. But I do actually have a modicum of common sense when I wish to use it, and I realize you were pissed over my part in the whole mess. I judged you based on a set of preconceived ideas I had about you. I thought I knew what you were all about, and I treated you accordingly. What I should have done right in the beginning was tell you your father was ill and ask you to come home. Believe it or not, that *was* what I originally intended to do." He smiled gently.

A shiver ran through her. She could tell he felt it, too, when he tightened the grip on her hand.

"Forgive me, Justine. Come home with me. Please?"

"I lied," she whispered.

His fingers tensed. "About what?"

"It wasn't fucking. It was making love. And I was scared silly that you'd reject me in the end, so I made sure I did it first."

He let out a long sigh as if he'd been holding his breath. "Christ, I love you. I'll do anything you want just so you don't go back to the dillhole you worked for."

She laughed and sniffed. "Are you always going to eavesdrop on my phone calls?"

He cupped her face with a gentle hand. "Maybe. But if I do, I promise to ask first."

She turned her face into his touch and kissed the center of his palm. "I do believe I'm in love with you, too."

"Thank God. Will you marry me?"

"I do believe I will."

He pressed a soft kiss to her lips, tracing the seam with his tongue. God, she loved his tongue.

"Now, about the job."

"What job?"

"CFO. Will you take it when Harrison leaves? For me?"

"I thought that was just some bullshit you made up to get me to stay."

He rubbed her nose with his. "No. Harrison's leaving, and you're the perfect replacement."

"But you haven't even seen my resume."

"I know your worth without the piece of paper to prove it."

God. She loved a man who actually believed in her. She wondered if her father would fight Len on the appointment. Not that it mattered. Fifteen years ago she'd run away rather than stand up to him. But she was a woman now and running from the fight wasn't an option.

"What's the salary?"

He shot off a figure.

"And when do I get to be CEO?"

"Honey, as far as I'm concerned, you already are. You can order me around any time you want."

She smiled at the possibilities. "Then here's my first order."

She leaned over to whisper in his ear.

His eyes widened, their tempting shade darkening. "You want to do that *here*?"

"Well, not right here." She stroked his arm. "But you've got to admit that while you've complimented my blow job technique, I've never actually … you know."

He pinned her with a glittering gaze. "Made me come that way?"

She licked her lips and batted her eyelashes. "Swallowed."

His eyes widened appreciatively. "Holy shit."

"And, I know just the perfect spot for carrying out my little plan." She stroked his lips with her tongue and drank in his deeply satisfying groan. "It's on the way back home."

EPILOGUE

"Oh my God."

Justine tipped her head back, closed her eyes and savored the sensations. The tips of her fingers tingled and her toes spasmed.

"You really like it?" Len murmured against her ear, sending a shiver coursing down her spine.

"More. Give me more."

"My pleasure."

He reached around, picked up the bottle and poured her another glass of shimmering chardonnay bearing the Falcon label.

Four pairs of Falconer eyes watched, waited, breaths held and fingers crossed.

She drew in the gentle bouquet, then swirled the crisp yet delicate liquid on her tongue.

"Well, Ms. CEO?" her father prompted. Despite having recently retired his chairmanship of the Board of Jarreau-Falconer Wineries, he was as excited as the rest of them.

The taste was almost as delicious as one of those orgasms Len was so good at bestowing.

"Well?" Len pressed.

She looked at her husband and let her gaze soften. "I do believe you've created a work of art, sweetheart."

The man was truly an artist. In the bedroom, the boardroom, and the vineyard.

THE END

About The Author

Jasmine Haynes (who also writes for Liquid Silver Books as JB Skully) lives in the California mountains, and she's married to her very own Viking God. Gee, now isn't that a heroic image. She's been making up stories since she was six (her sister still remembers being forced to read those horrible early attempts). She loves writing hot, sexy romance, the stuff fantasies are made. Especially her own. For something no less hot but with a darker edge, try a JB Skully novel.

Visit Jasmine Haynes and JB Skully at their website http://www.skullybuzz.com

Liquid Silver Books

Visit Us For Other Distinctive and Sensual Romantic Erotica Reading

Happy Campers
Vanessa Hart – Contemporary Romance

Gray Webster is two weeks away from marrying another woman when he meets Leslie Turner. He blames his instant and intense attraction to Leslie on bridegroom jitters. His theory—and resistance—unravel when he finally gives in to temptation. And gives in and gives in…

It's All Relative
Dee S. Knight – Contemporary Romance

A smart and sassy Southern chef and restaurateur, Sally Jean is fully confident when creating a lavish feast for hundreds. But a sensual feast of herself for one man?

Business Or Pleasure … Or Both?
Duet Novel – Contemporary Romance

Enchantress
– Rae Morgan
Double The Pleasure
– Jasmine Haynes

More Than A Night
Jasmine Haynes – Contemporary Romance

All Justine Jarreau wants in a one-night-stand is an uncomplicated, casual, mind-blowing sexual experience. And Len No-Last-Name seems like the perfect candidate to fulfill her fantasy.

Love Lessons
Vanessa Hart – Contemporary Romance

Wendy Powers has sworn off men. Busy with her career, she's been disappointed with the dating scene, so why bother?

Impatient Passion
Dee S. Knight – Contemporary Romance

Austin D. Gardner, an award-winning web designer in San Francisco, has just faced the fact that she is going to turn thirty-five years old on Saturday and her life is nowhere near what she dreamed it would be. She needs to make big changes.

The Cinderella Curse
Dee S. Knight – Contemporary Romance

One evening, in a land far away, a wife spins a fairy tale for the amusement of her husband. It's not your typical child's tale, of course, but an updated, more adult version of the classic, Cinderella.

Skin Deep
Jasmine Haynes – Contemporary Romance

Kirby Prescott is a woman in control of her life. She owns a thriving company, has her pick of gorgeous escorts, and no one to tell her what to do. And she has Jack Taylor, a man she's never met but who knows her more intimately than almost anyone.

Wild Knights
Blaise Kilgallen – Contemporary Romance

What thirty-seven year old, sex-deprived widow wouldn't welcome a hot fling with a younger, handsome hunk? Just ask Carla Moore.

Bittersweet
Louisa Trent – Contemporary Romance

While recuperating in Maine, edgy Boston police detective Cameron Wyler mistakes frustrated schoolteacher Gertrude Prescott for a hooker on the lam.

The Pickup Line
Louisa Trent – Contemporary Romance

…because sometimes all a man and woman really have in common is nothing, and sometimes nothing will keep them apart…

Weekend Games
Chris Tanglen – Erotic Thriller

On the first Friday of every month, Eric and Genevieve Fain join another married couple, David and Melissa, at their cabin in the woods for a weekend of sex games…

Some Rough Edge Smoothin'
Louisa Trent – Contemporary Romance

… sometimes sex is all a man and a woman really have in common, and sometimes that's more than enough …

True Seeing
Leigh Wyndfield – Paranormal

Susan Rivers has a problem. She can True See. This psychic ability has kept her from developing a close relationship with any man. After eleven months of resistance, Susan finally breaks down and goes to the man of her dreams' apartment—and ends up experiencing an afternoon of passion beyond anything she could imagine.

Man Of Her Dreams
Dee S. Knight – Paranormal

Cassandra Hudson dreams, just like everyone else. But sometimes Cassandra's dreams foretell events. And now she's experiencing the most debilitating recurring nightmare yet, centering around a tall man with deep, blue eyes. And her husband, who's been dead two years.

Touch Me
Louisa Trent – Paranormal

A beautiful witch in sexual bondage; a beleaguered warrior carnally enthralled; centuries of recriminations and lust explode when a past wrong is confronted.

Dead To The Max
Book 1 of the Max Series
JB Skully – Paranormal

"Dead to the Max" is the fast-paced adventure of the irrepressible Max Starr, a thirty-something, down on her luck accountant with the unfortunate gift of being psychic.

Destiny's Magick
Rae Morgan – Paranormal

Drake Morgan is a witch. He is also the leader of the largest and most powerful coven in the United States. As he fights enemies, both without and within, he continues his search for the one woman, his complement, who can help him protect his people from the dark machinations of a twisted follower of chaos magick.

Waiting For You
Glenda Diana – Paranormal

A world where mortals have never dared to tread, where time has no meaning, where things are not always as they appear, where war comes and death awaits those unlucky to lose in battle, and where two societies exist beyond the fabric of human concepts.

John The Deliverer
Book 1 of the Raven Series
Rhiannon Neeley – Vampire Romance

"John the Deliverer" tells the tale of John Raven, long-time vampire hunter, who is sent by the lead vampire, Devlin Morse, to find out more about author Madison Woods.

Captive
Louisa Trent – Historical Romance

In the year 1100 on the Scottish borderlands, a brooding warrior with enormous sexual appetites succumbs to the powerful forces of his dark nature when he abducts a novitiate in a plan to avenge his wife's death.

Portal
Sydney Morgann – Science Fiction Romance

An erotic space romp that will have you holding your sides with laughter while panting for sexual release.

Yesterday's Secret Sins
Marilyn Lee – Romantic Suspense

The last thing Dylan Mitchell wanted was an affair with a woman fourteen years his junior, who already had more money than he could hope to earn in a lifetime as a police chief. Yet the moment he meets aspiring writer Kristine Matthews, his life is turned upside down. Despite himself, he's furious and defensive one moment, and tender and horny the next.

A Dangerous Attraction
Lisa Renee Jones – Romantic Suspense

The woman he can't have is the one he wants… Sam has wanted Meagan from the moment he first set eyes on her. She is a sweet little contradiction who tempts him like no other. Her eyes say she wants him, but her words lash out at him…

Afternoon Delights – Volume 1
Short Story Anthology
Ten sensual stories by ten Liquid Silver authors

From ancient worlds and vampire realms to isolated islands and the wild beauty of the Amazon, revisit old flames, kindle new ones, explore contemporary relationships and indulge your fantasies.

Shut Up And Drive!
Quick Silver – Short
Dakota Cassidy – Contemporary Romance

What if the man you just picked up turned out to be the answer to your every sensual fantasy? A broken-down car and a hot guy who needs a lift, plus an overwhelming urge to set aside the constraints of everyday life, turn Tess' trip through the desert into a ride along a road leading to bliss!